ALSO BY NEIL McGAUGHEY

OTHERWISE KNOWN AS MURDER

SCRIBNER

NEW YORK LONDON TORONTO SYDNEY TOKYO SINGAPORE

AND THEN THERE WERE TEN

A Stokes Moran Mystery

NEIL McGAUGHEY

•

SCRIBNER
1230 Avenue of the Americas
New York, NY 10020

DESIGNED BY DIANE STEVENSON/SNAP-HAUS GRAPHICS

Manufactured in the United States of America

1   3   5   7   9   10   8   6   4   2

Library of Congress Cataloging-in-Publication Data
McGaughey, Neil.
And then there were ten: a Stokes Moran mystery / Neil McGaughey.
p.   cm.
I. Title.
PS3563.C36372A84   1995
813'.54—dc20
94–44395
CIP

ISBN 0-684-19760-X

For Randall Allen Lee
August 14, 1952—June 25, 1978
First friend of childhood, forever alive in memory

ACKNOWLEDGMENTS

Once again, I am indebted to Nancy and Nolan Minton for their assistance during the evolution of this project from rough idea to finished manuscript.

I would also like to express my appreciation to Phil Holdman of the Browsers and to Steve Hale of the Hollywood USO Mobile Shows for their assistance in researching the Hollywood Canteen, and to Dr. John Cook for his advice on medical details.

For their constant support and encouragement, I extend special thanks to Kathie Adams, Lynn Clark, Sue Hathorn, Orley Hood, Jane Lee, Mark Smith, and Shirley Tipton.

I cannot end this note without mentioning the invaluable input of both my agent, Martha Kaplan, and my editor, Susanne Kirk.

And last, but never least, a special nod to Don.

AND THEN THERE WERE
TEN

CHAPTER 1

"The most refreshing aspect
of this entire series
is its complete
and total rejection
of serious intent."

—Stokes Moran,
on Lilian Jackson Braun's
The Cat Who Went into the Closet

$\mathcal{B}$ootsie found the body.

It lay facedown, in the reeds at the water's edge. Even before I got close enough to identify what it was, I could tell something was wrong.

Bootsie never can keep a secret. Her half-bark, half-growl always lets me know when she has stumbled onto something interesting. Usually it's a frightened squirrel, or a turtle, or even a bug. Bootsie is a killer on bugs.

But this time, from the cautious way she was acting—first timidly nosing close, then suddenly leaping back—I figured it must be a snake. Snake? SNAKE!

Common sense should have told me that no snake would dare venture out in Connecticut in midwinter, especially not in these frigid January temperatures. But, at the moment, I was not thinking, just reacting.

"Bootsie," I yelled. "Get back!" I could just see her getting bitten by a snake. Then I could just as clearly picture sweeping the seventy-pound Irish setter up in my arms and carrying her on pounding legs the three blocks to Dr. Nancy Minton's animal hospital. I hoped to avoid both possibilities.

"Bootsie! Come here!" But Bootsie was studiously ignoring me.

I looked around for something, anything, with which to scare the snake away. Nothing. Not a stick, not a brick, not even a Frisbee. I had to remember to complain to the Tipton city fathers on how spotless they kept their river park.

I started running. Bootsie, as is her habit on our daily walks along the Yessula, had forged way ahead, and I still had to cover fifty yards—fifty interminable yards—to reach her. It seemed to take forever, but I was screaming every step of the way.

"Dog! Do you hear me? Come here! Now!" But Bootsie was edging ever closer to her quarry. I prayed, please God don't let anything happen to her—she doesn't mean any harm, she just doesn't know any better.

My breath in my ears and my heart in my throat, I finally reached the point where she stood overlooking the water. Not caring about the potential peril to me, I had only one thought—get her away from the danger.

I grabbed at her tail and yanked her back toward me. Hard. Bootsie growled and showed her teeth. Bootsie likes to pretend she's nobody's pushover, but she'd never bite me. She just doesn't like anyone messing with her backside.

I held her against my heaving chest, grateful I had rescued her in time. I covered her head with kisses. She struggled free and peered at me as if I'd lost my senses. Then she barked and turned back toward the water.

"Oh, no you don't." I lurched forward and laced my fingers tightly around her leather collar. "Not this time, girl."

But Bootsie was pulling against me with all her weight, and, off balance as I was, I couldn't stop my forward momentum. I fell. Bootsie yelped and sidled out from under me. With nothing to stop my headlong descent, I slid face first down the frozen bank.

Somewhere amid spitting out the icy water and freeing my hands of the mud's suction, I spotted Bootsie's prize. Stupidly, I gave voice to the first inane thought that popped into my head.

"At least it's not a snake," I muttered.

CHAPTER 2

"Like a good hostess,
the author
makes sure there's something
here for every taste."

—Stokes Moran,
on Carolyn G. Hart's *Southern Ghost*

$\mathcal{L}$ee and I had returned from New Orleans on the first day of the new year, fully expecting to be married by the end of the month. You might say that was our joint New Year's resolution. Along with my giving up smoking again, as Lee pointedly reminded me. And reminded me ad nauseam.

"If I can do it, you can do it," she said, as we sat at her kitchen table. The taxi from Kennedy had deposited us on her doorstep in Manhattan less than half an hour previously, and the first thing both of us had wanted was a cup of coffee. And then another.

Lee stood up, took her coffee cup over to the percolator, and poured a refill. She queried me with a look, but I shook off the offer.

"You had gone six months without one," Lee continued her chastisement as she poured generous amounts of cream and sugar into her mug, "then you had to start up again."

"Don't you think you had a little something to do with that?" I gently teased. "After all, it was the New Orleans adventure* that started me smoking again."

But Lee would not take the bait. She had stopped smoking, and had stuck to it. For the grand total of seven months.

"You can't get off the hook that easily," she said. "Nobody forced you to put that weed back in your mouth. You made that decision all on your own." No one's more sanctimonious, or more constantly irritating, than a reformed smoker.

I sighed, and said I'd think about it.

"You'd better do more than think about it," said Lee. She walked back to where I remained seated, reached around me to place her freshly made cup of coffee on the tabletop, and began to massage my shoulders. "I don't want a husband who dies of lung cancer."

"How about a husband who dies of heart failure, or gets run over crossing the street, or gets murdered in Central Park?" I said.

"No, thank you," Lee answered. "Give me a husband who dies of old age." She draped her arms around me, resting her chin on the top of my head. I felt her jaw move as she reiterated, "Very old age."

I tilted my head back, reached up, pulled her head down

Otherwise Known as Murder (Scribner, 1994).

to mine, and kissed her. "I like that demise best, too."

We both laughed.

* * *

The next morning I took Lee's Land Rover down to John Street, where Mark Crews had been dog-sitting Bootsie for almost a week. Lee had decided to remain in Manhattan for a couple of days, tying up what she called "some major loose ends." Even if I was soon to become her husband, I had to remind myself that she was agent to more than just Stokes Moran.

For the uninformed, I write nationally syndicated mystery reviews under that pseudonymous byline. Currently, under the Stokes Moran name, my reviews appear in more than eighty newspapers, Sunday supplements, and mystery fanzines all across the country. My real name is Kyle Malachi, and it's a name I much prefer to the ingratiatingly pompous one I created. Hate it though I may, the name Stokes Moran has become a recognized authority on mystery fiction, and I can't afford to drop it. Nobody would pay any attention to a Kyle Malachi review.

And pay is indeed what it's all about. I am compensated handsomely for my opinions. And after almost ten years, I still can't figure out why.

Last fall, with a lot of prompting and cajoling from Lee, I finally decided to try my hand at writing a mystery novel. But my manuscript still languished unfinished in the bowels of my computer. With the assistance of some cooperative publishers who had willingly sent me reading copies well in advance of scheduled publication, I had intentionally built up half a year's worth of reviews just to clear the time to write the damned thing. But the more time that went by, and the more consideration I gave the project, the more I became convinced that I should stick to the reading of mysteries. And leave the writing of them to the Tony Hillermans, Sarah Shankmans, Robert B. Parkers, and Carolyn G. Harts of this world. They, at least, knew what they were doing.

I chuckled. But there was one advantage I enjoyed over those mystery greats, I admitted to myself. Book or no book, I had an agent who wanted all of me, not just the standard fifteen percent. Where I was concerned, Lee gave author representation a whole new meaning.

* * *

I fought the morning rush-hour traffic all the way to John Street. After enduring Bootsie's copyrighted wet welcome, I thanked Mark, stashed Bootsie in the back with the luggage, and headed off to Tipton, Connecticut. And home.

* * *

The sight of the familiar gray wood and stone house at the end of the quiet cul-de-sac never fails to set my heart racing. I can think of no other feeling that is quite so comforting, quite so uplifting, as coming home. Especially when I've been away for awhile. It's pure unadulterated indescribable bliss.

Bootsie feels the same way. Even before I'd braked the

Land Rover to a stop, she had leaped out and gone to re-
claim her territorial rights. While I carted the suitcases up to
the front step, Bootsie sniffed and squatted, sniffed and
squatted, at various spots around the yard. With her actions,
she seemed to be sending a clear and unequivocal message.
Let any and all interloping canines beware—Bootsie was
back in town.

As soon as I threw open the door, the dog abandoned her external pursuits and bounded ahead of me, almost knocking the
luggage out of my hands in the process. With Bootsie happily
occupied reestablishing contact with her world, I stashed the
bags in the downstairs closet and went to retrieve the box I'd
kept next to me in the Land Rover's front seat.

I balanced it carefully in my arms, cradling it as I had all
the way from New Orleans, through two taxi rides and one
long flight. I had not allowed it out of my immediate vicinity
the entire trip. This little cardboard box contained a treasure
beyond imagination. I had purposely refused to think about
it. Until now.

As I kicked the front door closed behind me, I stood and
looked at the bookshelves lining the living-room walls. Over
five thousand books—mostly mysteries—that I had col-
lected over the past twenty years greeted my eyes.

I'm justifiably proud of my collection. I have a fairly representative selection of titles from nineteen fifty forward. And
for the past nine years—the period that I've been reviewing
mysteries—I possessed almost every important title.

But the books in the little cardboard box—which I now placed on the edge of my brass and glass cocktail table while I decided what to do with them—were a different matter indeed.

These were the cornerstones of the genre. *Farewell, My Lovely* and *The Little Sister* by Raymond Chandler. *Red Harvest* and *The Thin Man* by Dashiell Hammett. Cornell Woolrich's *The Bride Wore Black*, Agatha Christie's *The Mysterious Affair at Styles* and *The Pale Horse*, Dorothy L. Sayers' *Murder Must Advertise*, James M. Cain's *Double Indemnity*, S. S. Van Dine's *The Benson Murder Case*, Rex Stout's *Fer-de-Lance*, John Dickson Carr's *The Three Coffins*, and Ellery Queen's *The Roman Hat Mystery*. A baker's dozen of the greatest mysteries ever written. All with dust jackets, all in excellent condition. It was a collector's dream come true.

And now they belonged to me.

With loving hands, I pulled the top volume out of the box. Raymond Chandler's *Farewell, My Lovely*. I handled it gingerly, uncertain whether I'd ever before seen a copy of this title in its first-edition state. The dust jacket was beautifully preserved, the front cover drawing simple yet commanding. At the very top, a couple of small blue-gray clouds rested benignly against a solid rust background. Next came the word FAREWELL in block letters, the first four letters of the word a lighter rust than the ending four, all on an upward slant. Then, in white lowercase italic, *my lovely*. In the bottom quadrant, in a pristine script that matched the color of the clouds, came the author's name, followed by smaller block letters, also on an upward slant, that announced AUTHOR OF "THE BIG SLEEP".

Suddenly, I realized I had not taken a breath the entire time I had been holding the book in my hands. I carefully opened the flyleaf and read the first sentence of the dust jacket copy: "There is a hint of cruelty at the very beginning, a hint of a world in which viciousness is normal; and as the story develops, the atmosphere becomes increasingly malevolent and charged with evil." Odd, that's not exactly how I would have characterized the novel. I smiled. I guess publishers had overzealous copywriters even way back then. I glanced at the nineteen forty list price—two dollars. More than a half century later, that modest sixteen bits had multiplied some ten-thousandfold. If only the original buyers had known.

I closed the hinge and placed the book gently back in the box. It was simple—I would just have to build a special glass-encased shelf specifically for these books. Nothing else in my collection comes close to the value of these priceless volumes. I figured I'd have to increase my insurance as well. By how much? Fifty thousand? A hundred thousand? Or more?

I groaned. For titles such as Anne Rice's *Interview with the Vampire*, Sue Grafton's *"A" is for Alibi*, Sara Paretsky's *Indemnity Only*, and dozens of other mid- to late-twentieth-century acquisitions that had appreciated wildly in value, I carried adequate insurance. But these new additions would blow that coverage out of the water.

Just then, two things happened at once. Bootsie galloped into the room, swishing her plumed tail frantically, and knocked the treasured box to the floor, spilling its contents. And the telephone rang.

I yelled at the dog to calm down, ignored the phone, and bent to inspect the damage. None of the books looked the worse for the experience. I breathed a sincere sigh of relief, replaced all thirteen in the box, and set it safely in the middle of the table.

The phone continued to blare away, and I finally ended its peremptory and irritating summons.

"Hello," I bellowed.

"Mmmpf," Lee said. "Do you always answer the phone mad?"

"No." I softened my tone. "Bootsie knocked over the books, and I was trying to get them up off the floor, and the phone just kept ringing . . . Oh, never mind." I sighed. "I apologize."

"Good. I need you in a more receptive frame of mind, anyway."

"Uh-oh. That doesn't sound promising." Over the past few days, I had become increasingly familiar with Lee's—how shall I put it?—professional style of management.

"It's just that I need you to come back into Manhattan."

"I just got home," I protested.

"I know."

"And I'm tired."

"I know that, too. So am I."

I knew I could have kept offering excuses and Lee would

have kept agreeing sympathetically. But I also knew the eventual outcome.

"All right," I capitulated. "What is it?"

Lee hesitated. "A birthday party," she began.

"Oh, no," I complained. "I'm certainly not up to a party. Not tonight."

"It's Izzy's eightieth birthday. Kyle, you know I wouldn't ask if it were anyone else except Izzy, but you know how I feel about him."

I knew. Izzy Cohen was, for want of a better term, Lee's mentor. He had helped her get started as an agent back in the early eighties. She had often said she owed her career to Izzy Cohen.

"What with our little adventure in New Orleans and all," Lee was continuing, "it completely slipped my mind. But when I got back to my desk this morning, there it was on my calendar—circled in red—big as life."

"I guess you can't send your regrets."

"I really can't, darling. If we had still been out of town, that would have been different. But for me to be physically right here in New York and not show up, Izzy'd never forgive me. And I wouldn't be able to forgive myself either."

"Well, can't you go without me?" I offered.

"No, I can't." I could hear the petulance in Lee's voice. "I've been single for far too long. Besides, I want to show you off. And prove to some of those told-you-sos that I can snag a husband after all."

"You make me sound like a prize in a Cracker Jack box."

Lee laughed. "Oh, I regard you a little bit better than that. Will you come?" she asked, then added, "please?"

"I guess so," I grumbled. "What time do we have to be there?"

"The party starts at eight. And has to be over by ten. The invitation was very firm about that."

"Why?"

"Izzy's parties always end early. He's an early-to-bedder. Always has been."

Good, I thought. Tonight I intended to be one as well.

* * *

But things didn't quite turn out that way.

I was past eight o'clock getting to Lee's apartment on West Eighty-second Street. After Lee's phone call, I made the mistake of going next door to pick up my mail. My neighbor and friend, Nolan James, routinely collects my mail for me when I'm out of town. Nolan's a great guy, but you just can't shut him up. And today had been no exception.

"You sure do create a lot of bother," Nolan said, as he pulled a heavy cardboard box out of his entryway closet. It was so filled with envelopes and packages that the top flaps would not close. We stood in his open doorway, from which vantage point I could glance over to my own backyard where Bootsie was at play.

"UPS must have come by at least twice a day," he said.

"And I'm getting to know the FedEx lady so well I'm thinking of asking her out for a cup of coffee." He grinned.

I grinned back. "And what about the United States Postal Service? Did you forget about them?"

"No way. Mr. Fairman says he's going to have to take early retirement from all the extra weight you add to his bag."

I tried to lift the box, but it felt as if it weighed at least a hundred pounds. Nolan laughed. "See what I mean? There's more this time than ever before. You having some kind of book orgy?"

I gave up on my efforts to move the box. "This is the first time I've been gone for more than three days at a time. Plus it's that time of the month."

Nolan grinned. "I didn't know a man could get that."

It took me a moment to catch his joke. "No," I finally said, ignoring his comedy routine, "these are probably a lot of the new spring releases. After the holidays, publishers get back to serious business."

Nolan leaned against the front-door frame. Thin and lanky, he had close-cropped dark hair and a pockmarked complexion, probably resulting from losing a teenage battle with acne. Compared to me, he was a few pounds lighter, a couple of inches shorter, and several years older, since I presumed he was fast approaching fifty while I had just turned forty.

"You came back right before Christmas," he said, "but you didn't come over to pick up your stuff. Then you took off again. With a good-looking young lady in tow. You holding out on your old buddy?"

"That was my agent."

"Oh." Nolan's voice was so flat it would have made a La Guardia runway seem bumpy.

"You don't believe me?"

"She stayed the night."

"That's right. She stayed the night." With Nolan, nosiness is a way of life. A retired cop, he had learned his observation skills well. And was not about to abandon them, in or out of the force.

"Are you contracting out now to the FBI?" I asked.

"No, just asking."

I finally relented. "Lee and I are getting married. Is that what you wanted to hear?"

The smile filled his face. "Congratulations, old buddy. I knew someday some little girl would grab that brass ring."

"It's supposed to be gold, in case you've forgotten."

"With a piker like you, she oughta be grateful for brass."

We both laughed. Nolan's such a good friend, plus he's so willing to help me out, that I rarely mind his intrusive attitude. We stood in his doorway and talked for a few more minutes, then he and I both carried the heavy box over to my house.

As he was leaving, he added, "You let me know next time you go out of town, you hear?"

"Don't worry," I answered, "I'm not planning any more trips. I've had my fill of travel. For quite a while." As they say, famous last words.

* * *

The mail would just have to wait. There were at least fifty packages, varying in size from small to jumbo extra-large, too many to sort through in the time remaining before I had to get ready for my evening with Lee. But, on second thought, surely I could look through just a few of the letters. That little chore certainly wouldn't take too long.

A few bills, addressed to Kyle Malachi. Dozens of publicity releases, addressed to Stokes Moran. Half a dozen magazines. A handwritten envelope finally caught my attention.

Opening it, I found a request from an editor of an upcoming mystery anthology asking if I would list my ten all-time favorite mystery novels. He was surveying leading figures in the mystery world and felt my inclusion would be noteworthy.

"He sure knows how to get what he wants," I muttered. "But he's barking up the wrong tree with me." However, even with that initial dismissal, I must admit the proposition intrigued me.

My ten all-time favorite mystery novels. I normally don't believe in lists. For one thing, my favorite mystery novel is usually the one I've just finished reading. Trying to cull ten from a lifetime of reading pleasure seemed impossible. A hundred, maybe. Perhaps even fifty. But ten? I didn't think it could be done.

And, then, without realizing it, I began compiling the list.

"There'd have to be at least one Christie," I said to myself. But which one? *The Murder of Roger Ackroyd* is generally regarded as her masterpiece. But I've always preferred *Murder on the Orient Express* or *The ABC Murders* or *Murder in Retrospect*. But don't forget *What Mrs. McGillicuddy Saw!*, I reminded myself. Or *Death on the Nile*. That would be a good choice. It was reportedly one of Christie's own favorites, and it was one that still gave me pleasure in later rereadings.

But what about *The Mysterious Affair at Styles*? That would certainly be representative, since it was her first novel.

I finally decided on *Curtain*. The book is not generally regarded as one of the author's best achievements, but it is an essential Christie title since it deals with the death of Hercule Poirot, her great Belgian detective. And, of course, the plot and setting are uniquely typical of her genius. Plus, it's one of my favorites. And that's the whole purpose of this exercise, isn't it?

Yes, I thought, *Curtain* it shall be. One down, only nine to go. Satisfied, I looked at my watch. Where had the time gone? I yelled Bootsie in from outside and rushed up the stairs, throwing off my clothes as I went. Oh my god, was Lee ever going to pitch a fit!

* * *

Lee's fit lasted all the way to Izzy Cohen's front door. He lived in a three-story brownstone on Manhattan's East Side somewhere in the Sixties. I never did get the exact address since Lee had urgently blared the information at the driver while I was still in the process of entering the cab, barely getting my door closed before the taxi screeched out into the evening traffic.

What that poor Iranian driver must have thought of us! Lee never stopped lecturing the whole way.

"I told you Izzy likes to go to bed early," she said as the cab lurched to a stop. Lee shoved open the door, peremptorily handed the driver a ten-dollar bill to cover the fare. "And now," she continued as we both gained the sidewalk, "you've made it impossible for us to visit with Izzy for more than a few minutes."

I glanced at my watch. It was almost ten. "If he says anything about you being late," I said as we started up the steps, "just blame me."

Lee's incessant harangue irritated me. Why was she carrying on so? Was this how she normally behaved? Was this the woman I was planning to marry?

The front door opened, and an elderly woman walked out. I lunged to catch the door before it closed and almost knocked over the stooped lady in the process. She uttered a mild oath and scurried down the steps. I frowned in belated recognition.

"Was that Katharine Hepburn?" I asked Lee as we entered the foyer.

"What?"

"That lady just now. Was that Katharine Hepburn?" I repeated.

"It could have been," answered Lee as she shrugged out

of her coat and handed it to the attendant. "I didn't get a good look, but since Izzy knows everybody in the entertainment business, it wouldn't be surprising to find Katharine Hepburn here."

"Damn," I said, "and I almost knocked her down."

"Well, I'm sure she's survived much worse treatment," said Lee, as we climbed the stairs.

"You're in a strange mood tonight," I said. "First you overreact to my being late, and now you dismiss Katharine Hepburn as casually as you would a termite."

Lee stopped on the landing and gave me an exasperated look. "Kyle, I'm sorry. It's just that things aren't going at all as I planned."

"What things?" I asked, confused.

"We should have taken Izzy's private elevator," Lee said. She started climbing a second flight of stairs, with me following right on her heels.

"What things?" I repeated. "What plan? What are you keeping from me?"

"Izzy wants to talk to you," she finally admitted.

Instead of clarifying, Lee was just making things more muddled.

"Talk to me?" I asked, surprised. "Why does a man I never met want to talk to me?"

"That's what I was going to tell you. But you would have to be late. Tonight of all nights. And I had to wait. And the longer I waited, the madder I got. Then when you finally did show up, I couldn't think straight, I was so angry."

I grabbed her shoulder and turned her to face me. Her shoulder-length brunette curls shimmered under the light from the golden chandeliers. "Lee, you're not making any sense," I said.

"I know." She shook off my hand. "I don't have time to explain now. Just play along. With whatever Izzy says."

"What do you mean, just play along?"

"I can't go into it now. We're here," she announced. "I'll tell you later."

As we topped the last stair, I saw dozens of people jammed into the third-floor hallway. Since at five feet tall, Lee barely reaches my chin, I tried to stick close to her, but the crush of bodies soon proved that impossible. Stretching to my full six-foot height, I peered over the heads in front of me, attempting to keep Lee in sight, locking my eyes as best I could on the blue silk dress she was wearing. But eventually I lost that identification as well.

Which left me lost in a sea of strange faces.

I take that back. I certainly hadn't before met any of these people, but many of the faces weren't strange at all. In fact, they were quite familiar. As well as famous.

I spotted numerous celebrities, new and old alike. The tall man with his elbow resting on a lady's head. Wasn't that what's-his-name? Oh, you know, the star of those spaghetti westerns from the sixties.

And the woman on whose hair his elbow rested. Wasn't she the actress who was married to Howard Hughes at one time? Or was it Donald Trump?

I gave up trying to put names to the famous faces. I knew I'd seen them, either in movies or on talk shows or in the tabloids. I exchanged words with a few as I macheted my path through the throng.

"What are we doing here?" The rhetorical question, spoken aloud after a particularly frustrating maneuver past a gargantuan beast of a man—wasn't he the star of those Exterminator movies?—was nevertheless answered.

"We're waiting for our audience with the king," said a woman who looked remarkably like Gilda Radner doing her classic Baba Wawa routine.

"King?" I gasped into the air pocket that we shared.

She thumbed toward the door against which she leaned. "Izzy's bedroom. Only one or two people are allowed in at any one time. You see, he's been on oxygen, the poor dear."

"What?" I was having a hard time remaining vertical against the mob's ebb and flow. Plus, I could barely hear her words over the conversational roar.

"After all, he is eighty years old."

I felt I had missed something she'd said, but just then Izzy's bedroom door opened and Lee popped out.

"Wow, am I glad to see you," I said. "It's been a nightmare out here."

Lee barely acknowledged my presence. She took a deep breath and then screamed, putting all of her hundred or so pounds into the effort. My ears ringing, I barely heard her shouted statement that Izzy would not receive any more visitors.

Her announcement had an immediate and profound result. The crowd dispersed, not gradually, but suddenly. One
minute, dozens of people were packed in that tiny hallway;
the next, Lee and I stood there alone.

Lee reached up, pulled my head down, and kissed me on
the left cheek. "Kyle, Izzy wants to talk to you alone. Please,
do this for me," she said mysteriously. "I'll explain everything when you get back to my place, I promise." She
backed away from me, then turned and sprinted toward the
stairs. "Don't worry about me," she called over her right
shoulder, "I'll grab a cab."

"Wait!" I yelled, starting after her. I made it as far as the
banister, but Lee had already disappeared. "What's this all
about?" I shouted at the empty air.

I heard her voice float up to me from the floor below.
"You'll find out."

Puzzled, wildly confused, feeling the total fool, but nevertheless intrigued, I turned and walked back down the hallway.

"Here goes nothing," I muttered and tapped lightly
against the closed bedroom door. I heard a responding grunt
that I interpreted as an invitation. I turned the knob and entered Izzy Cohen's inner sanctum.

CHAPTER 3

"The author
has created an enduring
and endearing
character—one who is
all the more disarming for his
incompetence."

—Stokes Moran,
on Parnell Hall's *Shot*

"Come in, Mr. Moran."

I expected to find a bedridden invalid; instead I found a man standing by the window, brandy snifter in hand. I closed the door behind me.

Izzy Cohen walked toward me, shifted his drink to his left hand, and extended his right hand in greeting. Again he surprised me; his grip was firm and steady.

"You seem shocked, Mr. Moran. Not what you expected, huh?"

"Well, it's just . . . " I fumbled for the right words.

"Please have a seat." He motioned to the sofa opposite the bed, propping himself against the bedstead.

"I thought you were . . . " Again, I had trouble finding the phrase.

"Feeble? Sick? Dying?" Izzy Cohen laughed, a high-pitched hyenalike cackle.

"Well, in a word, yes," I answered.

"You can see for yourself. What do you think?"

I thought Izzy Cohen definitely looked his eighty years. His skin, the part I could see beyond the elegant dressing gown he wore, hung loosely on his bones and had the translucence of fine satin. I supposed he had once been a man of some physical height, possibly six feet or more. Now he seemed shrunken and stooped. His face was wrinkled and liver-spotted. Only his eyes, a clear and lively blue, seemed out of place in the emaciated body.

"Well?" he asked, when I was too slow to respond.

"It's just that Lee said—"

"And she was right," he interrupted. "I had an attack of emphysema earlier today. Had to have the old oxygen." He nodded toward the tank and tent standing next to the bed. "That's what comes from almost seventy years of smoking." He reached in the pocket of his gown and pulled out a pack of Viceroys. "Would you care for a cigarette?" Again, the hyenalike laugh as he placed the cigarette between his lips.

"I'm trying to quit," I said.

"Good for you, young man." He lit the cigarette and then shook the flame from the match. "As you can see, I'm not a very good patient. My doctor can't believe I continue to smoke. He doesn't understand it's no longer a matter of choice. But I say what the hell, they ain't killed me yet."

I smiled, not knowing what else to say.

He took a long drag on the cigarette, then coughed the smoke out.

I stood up. "Mr. Cohen, are you all right?"

The hyena laughter mixed with the hacking cough. "Yes," he gasped. He waved me back into my seat. "And please, call me Izzy," he added between wheezes.

After a moment, the coughing spasm eased. He took a gulp of his drink.

"Where are my manners? Mr. Moran, you'll have to forgive me. Let me get you a brandy."

"Please, no," I answered. "I'm not much of a drinker."

Izzy walked to the bedside table and refilled his glass. Then he came and joined me on the sofa. He leaned back against the cushions, stretched, and sighed.

"I really wasn't up to seeing people tonight. I know I'm not acting like it, but I do try to take care of myself. And being in a room with a lot of people just seems to take all the oxygen out of the air. Know what I mean?"

I remembered the close confines of the cramped hallway and nodded understanding. He smiled, and I could see the years of tobacco use on his teeth and lips.

"I hated to miss the party," he continued. "At my age, you never know if another one will come around." Again, that signature laugh.

When the laugh died, silence followed. I had no idea why I was here, no inkling as to what he wanted. I felt uneasy, uncomfortable. His next words echoed my thoughts.

"You're probably wondering why I asked to see you?"

"Frankly, sir, I was."

"What did Lee tell you?"

"Very little, I'm afraid. Just that you wanted to talk to me," I said. Then I added, with as much emphasis as I could muster, "Alone."

Izzy nodded. "Good. I told her not to say a word. Not that she could have offered you much more than that, anyway."

"I'm afraid I don't understand," I said.

He shook his head. "Of course you don't, my boy." He stood up and walked over to the bed, then turned and faced me. "No way you could."

Again, I didn't know what to say, so I said nothing. But this time, neither did he. Izzy just stood there looking down at me. Finally, he spoke.

"I told Lee I needed help. I didn't tell her what it was, just that I couldn't go to the police, and that I didn't want to trust it to a private investigator. That's when she suggested you."

"Me?" I was dumbstruck.

Izzy misinterpreted my response. "Yes, yes, I know you're not a professional. But Lee tells me you're quite a good amateur detective. And most of all, she assures me you'll be discreet."

What had Lee done? I now knew why Izzy was calling me by my Moran name, but had Lee taken leave of her senses? An amateur detective? "But I'm not—" I started.

"Not what? Not discreet?" Izzy barked out another cackle.

"No, no, I didn't mean that."

Izzy walked back to the sofa, sat down next to me, and patted my knee. "Look, I know you two are getting married."

I nodded.

"And I know you don't want anything to interfere with that."

"Yes sir, but you misunderstand—"

"Believe me, Mr. Moran, I wouldn't burden you with this for all the world. But I just don't have anywhere else to turn. You do understand, don't you?"

For some reason, Lee had put me in this awkward position. She had also told me to play along, to do it for her. Do what for her? What a simple metamorphosis—reviewer into gumshoe. Piece of cake. No problem. Right? Reading Chandler and Hammett had not quite prepared me for anything like this. A real person with a real problem. Was Lee insane?

Izzy tugged at my sleeve. "You will help me, won't you, Mr. Moran?"

Slowly, as if it were someone else's head moving, I nodded.

"Just call me Stokes," I said.

* * *

"What time is it?" Izzy asked.

I looked at my watch. "It's a little past ten," I answered.

He stood up, walked over to the window, and looked out at the city.

"It's starting to snow," he said. Even from where I sat on the sofa, I could see snowflakes reflected in the light from the streetlamps. Izzy turned back toward me.

"This is the first snow we've had since before Christmas. It's been a strange season."

For a time, Izzy just stood silently silhouetted against the window, staring, it seemed, not at me but through me. Beyond me. Perhaps no longer aware that I was in the room at all. Finally his reverie broke.

"Lee tells me you're a book person, so maybe you'll appreciate the irony. For years, publishers have been hammering at my door, eager to sign up my memoirs. I've always turned them down. Flat." Izzy turned back to the window and leaned his head against the pane. "Memoirs. Memories. A lifetime of memories. Little do they know."

Abruptly, he whirled around. "That's not what they want," he said, his voice more animated. "Super Agent to the Stars. That's more what they have in mind. They want dirt and gossip, sex and scandal." The hyena cackled. "And I could give it to them. Boy, could I ever! But at what price? To me? To my friends? To the people I've loved?"

Izzy sat against the edge of the bed. "Contrary to Lee's opinion, I'm not Saint Izzy. I've done a lot of things in my life I'd like to change. You don't get ahead in this business being Mr. Nice Guy. I've hurt a lot of people in the last fifty years. Helped some, of course—I don't want this to sound maudlin. But it's what some people would consider the bad things that you have to know about now.'"

I shifted in my seat. "Mr. Cohen, I don't think—"

He held up his hand. "Izzy, remember. And I don't want you to think. Not yet. I just want you to listen. To a story I never thought I'd tell, or ever want to tell, or ever have to tell."

"But I'm a stranger to you," I protested.

"All the better. It's not quite as painful that way. This is not something I could ever tell Lee, though you can certainly share any or all of it with her. I wouldn't want my secrets to come between you." He smiled. "But I just couldn't talk to her about it. You'll understand why in a moment."

Izzy walked over to where I sat, lifted my left arm, and glanced at my watch. "Ten fifteen," he announced. "I hope you don't have any plans. It's going to be a long night."

I thought about Lee waiting at her apartment, about Nolan dog-sitting with Bootsie, about the physical toll the last few days had taken on my body, about my bed in Tipton.

"No. No plans at all," I answered. "But I still don't understand—"

Izzy interrupted. "You will, my boy, you will. I think I'm going to lie down." He walked over to the bed and sat on the edge. "Are you comfortable where you are?"

I nodded. "But what is this all about?" I asked.

"Oh, didn't I mention that?" Izzy lifted his feet off the floor and stretched out on top of the bedcovers. "It's about blackmail."

CHAPTER 4

*"If this is really
how the other half lives
(and dies),
give me the good old middle class
anytime."*

—Stokes Moran,
on Edward Stewart's *Deadly Rich*

*I*zzy's narrative—

Or the likelihood of blackmail, that is. But let me start at the beginning.

I've dreamt this moment, I've dreaded this moment, I've hoped this moment would never come. I should have died with these words silent on my lips. But I've heard them in my mind so often it'll be like delivering a Shakespearean soliloquy. So I guess since the moment has finally arrived, it just means I've lived too long. At least five years too long, I'd say. Maybe even ten.

For some reason, I've always been struck by the words Charles Dickens wrote at the start of *David Copperfield*— "To begin my life with the beginning of my life, I record that I was born." Remember? *Izzy chuckled.* Well, don't worry.

I'm not going back quite that far. But I do think you need to know that I grew up in Jersey, just across the river from here. Jewish family, of course. Orthodox, though the religious aspect of it was never that important to me. Hated it, really. Strange, though, the older I get, the more I find myself thinking about it, finding comfort in it.

But that's neither here nor there. It's the family I want you to know about. Tight, close-knit, I guess like all Jewish families, or maybe just families in general, I don't know. Protected their own, looked out for each other. If one member found a good thing, he let his relatives in on it.

I had an uncle. Moe, can you believe it? Short for Moishe, I think. Though I never heard anybody call him anything but Moe. Izzy, by the way, is short for Isidore. You can't get much more Jewish than those two names. Somebody made a movie a few years ago called *Izzy and Moe*. It was not about me and my uncle, I can assure you of that.

Moe went out to California in the nineteen twenties and got in tight with Sam Goldwyn. Another Jew, see what I mean?

Early days, of course. Still the silents. Worked his way into the front office. Became Sam's right-hand man.

When I was twenty-four—let's see, that was the late thirties—Uncle Moe sent for me. It seemed one of Sam's stars—Moira McDonald—strange combination, you wouldn't remember her, of course. Well, she was causing problems. Didn't like the contract Goldwyn had her tied to. Wanted to renegotiate. Wanted her own agent. Moe told Sam I could be that agent. That way Sam could make little Moira happy, and still remain in control of the situation. Without her knowing about it, of course.

I didn't have the least notion of what being an agent meant. But Sam and Moe built me up to the little star. Told her I was a bigwig on the East Coast. My job in Jersey at that moment was hawking shoes door-to-door.

But I went West. Moe told me the concessions Goldwyn was willing to make. I presented them to Moira, with absolutely no confidence that she'd accept them. But she went along, eagerly, thought she had won the day. And I was on my way. Super Agent to the Stars. As easy as that.

I acquired another client, then another one after that. And I discovered that I had a knack for negotiating, the first thing in my life I was ever really good at. I also discovered I had a taste for the Hollywood life.

But while all these good things were happening to me in America, some very bad things were happening in other parts of the world. Hitler had already started his reign of terror, and his anti-Semitism began to claim real victims. People I knew, family members, suddenly disappeared without a trace. Uncles, aunts, cousins, friends, either ran for their lives or became targets for his bullies.

When Britain and France declared war on Germany, I went to London, determined to join the RAF, to fight the bloody Nazis. But the Brits wouldn't take me, found I had a heart murmur as well as hypertension. I even tried to bribe my way in, little good it did me. And I tried to join up again when America finally got into it. But I didn't fare any better with Uncle Sam than I had with Mother England. Bitterest disappointment in my life, not being in on the action.

But the war left Hollywood wide open. Many of the leading men enlisted. Suddenly there were openings for a new Clark Gable, the next Jimmy Stewart, so on like that. And I signed up many of those wannabees, some of whom went on to become major stars in their own right.

It's a tragic irony that the worst event in Jewish history indirectly helped make me the most successful agent in Hollywood history. Only in America, right? *Izzy cackled again.*

Which brings me to the point in my story beyond which there is no turning back.

Izzy lapsed into silence. I said nothing. This was his show, his stage. He alone had to decide whether to continue. Nothing I could offer would either persuade or discourage him. Finally, he continued.

You'll probably find this hard to believe—hah, make that impossible, especially given our modern sensibilities—but I remained a virgin until I was thirty-three years of age. That's right, thirty-three. A thirteen-year-old virgin these days is a rarity.

It wasn't that I was naive. I knew what sex was. It just didn't interest me. Today they'd call it low testosterone, I guess. Back then, all I was concerned with was my career, making the biggest deals, representing the biggest stars.

Until November twenty-second, nineteen forty-five, that is.

The war had ended, and it was the final night for the Hollywood Canteen. Thanksgiving night, as a matter of fact. I know you've heard of the Hollywood Canteen. A USO facility staffed by celebrities. Off Sunset Boulevard, on Cahuenga. Bette Davis got it going.

Well, that Thursday was its last night. A lot of major stars were there. If I remember right, you had Bob Hope. Marlene Dietrich. Nelson Eddy. Rosalind Russell. Bette Davis and John Garfield, both of whom had been there at the start. And several of my top players as well.

I normally stayed away from the Canteen. All those men in uniform just reminded me of my frustrated attempts to join up. Anyway, civilians weren't allowed, and I normally didn't use my clout to force my way in. But that night, what the hell. The war was won, Hitler was dead, and it was the last hurrah for the Canteen, an institution that would never rise again. So, that night was a special occasion. A farewell. A happy ending.

I took one of my starlets—her name was Maggie Mason—yeah, I know, you've never heard of her, but she was a nice kid. Made only a couple of movies, found out the fast life wasn't for her, and ended up marrying her home-town sweetheart. But I digress.

Well, anyway, it was a real send-off that night. I never saw a place that jumping, not before and not since. Musta been thousands crowded into that little place. Army, Navy, Army Air Corps, Merchant Marine. You name it, if it had a uniform, it was there that night. And not just Americans. There were guys there from England, and Norway, Australia, Canada, New Zealand.

All the Allies, from all over the globe. The Canteen normally restricted the number they let in, but not that last night. They even ignored their normal midnight closing. The place was wide open, and everybody was allowed to celebrate.

So that's how I came to meet Lev Levin. I thought Lev had to be short for something; it wasn't. Turned out Levin was, though. Shortened from Levinski.

He was all of nineteen. Just been mustered out of the Sixth Army down in San Diego. He had been stationed in the Philippines as a photographer for the last year of the war. Just got in. Wanted to see Tinsel Town before heading back to Minneapolis.

I got all that in the first ten minutes. He liked to talk, especially about himself. While he talked, I watched. I watched his green eyes glint when he smiled. I watched his lips turn down in an unconscious frown whenever Maggie interrupted his conversation. I watched his long fingers tapping on the tabletop. I watched the golden hairs poking out from beyond the cuff of his too-long shirtsleeve. I watched the way he held his head, the set of his jaw, his mannerisms, his movements. I watched everything about him.

At the ripe old age of thirty-three, I fell in love.

With a man yet.

I know this is hard for you to believe, but until that moment I didn't realize I was homosexual. As I told you earlier, I just thought I didn't have a sex drive. But all the emotion, all the passion I didn't think I had, surfaced in that instant. And it shocked me.

It was like a dam had burst inside me, and I was flooded with desire, drowning in it, suffocating in it. I could hardly breathe. His hand brushed against mine, and I almost passed out. I've never felt more exposed in my life. It was like I was wearing a neon sign on my forehead that was blinking out these brand-new feelings to everyone around me.

Of course, I know that wasn't the case. Maggie was too self-absorbed to notice anything or anyone but herself. And the other people around us didn't matter.

Sometime around midnight, Maggie's roommate joined us and brought with her a couple of sailors. Within half an hour, Maggie, her roommate, and the two sailors were gone, leaving Lev and me together. Alone. I know it sounds strange that in a room of a thousand people you could feel alone, but I did.

Lev kept up his monologue. I would occasionally grunt or insert a word here or there, but mostly he did all the talking. His eyes bored into mine, his words droned in my ears. I didn't know or understand what was happening, or would happen. I existed just for that one second, that one minute, that one hour.

But I've never felt more alive, more alert. I remember everything. The garlic and grease smells coming from the kitchen, the rattling of the dishes as the celebrities cleared the tables, the red checkerboard tablecloths, the music.

Ah, the music. They had real songs back then, not like the trash you hear today. "I'll Be Seeing You." "The White Cliffs of Dover." "Beyond the Blue Horizon." "A Nightingale Sang in Berkeley Square." Those were magical tunes. It was a magical time.

Lev and I closed the place. I didn't know what else to do. Since I was older, maybe Lev was waiting for some kind of signal from me. But I didn't know how to give a signal, or what kind of a signal to give.

We walked out to the parking lot, and without any discussion, Lev got into my old prewar Packard with me, and we drove back to my house. When we met, I assumed Lev Levin was Jewish, like me. But back at my place, I discovered, in the most wonderful manner imaginable, that he wasn't. Later, I found out that his father had emigrated from Poland in nineteen twenty and that Levinski was a Polish name. Not Jewish.

Lev was nineteen when we met; I was thirty-three. And our relationship lasted for forty-two years. But it's a wonder we survived at all.

The first few years were fine. I had a thriving agency and had picked up a lot of old stars back from the war. So many, in fact, that I had to hire additional staff to handle them all. I became big business—the Cohen Talent Agency, Inc. The studios were cranking out more movies than ever, and I had some of the hottest properties in town.

I managed to get Lev a job at Warner's as an assistant cameraman. Early on, he was pretty happy. A starstruck kid from the Midwest, he now spent every day on soundstages with some of the biggest stars in Hollywood. But at night, he'd have to stay home while I wheeled and dealed and partied with the big boys. There was no way I could include him. Remember, this was the late forties. Homosexuality ended careers. Period.

I didn't know it at the time, of course, but our relationship was a fairly open secret. Hollywood is a pretty closed community, and it doesn't take a genius to figure out what's going on when two men live together.

And suddenly my eyes were opened to other homosexual activity going on as well. Before the thunderbolt hit me that night in the Canteen, I had been totally blind to what was happening all around me. A few years ago Elizabeth Taylor made the rash statement that homosexuality created Hollywood. I had never thought of it exactly that way, but she was dead on target. Even after the disclosures of the last decade, the American public would still be in shock if they understood the enormity of what Elizabeth meant. If the homosexual ratio is one man in ten nationally, and I happen to think it's higher than that, then the ratio in Hollywood is one in two. And it wasn't that much different back in the early days, either.

And this startling realization on my part came about simply as a result of having Lev in my life.

But Lev didn't like being left out, and eventually this took its toll on our relationship.

It was New Year's Eve nineteen forty-eight. Once again I had to leave Lev at home while I went out to see and be seen. Except that night I didn't. I had planned a surprise. To hell with convention, Lev and I were doing the town.

I left the house as usual. Drove down to Tiny Naylor's for

a cup of coffee. Waited about thirty minutes before I headed back. I knew Lev would be bowled over at my surprise.

But the surprise was on me. I found him in bed with another man. Considering the advanced state of their activity, I could hardly have been out of the driveway before the other man arrived. I was livid.

We had a gigantic row. The worst fight we'd ever had, either before or after. Every instinct in me said to throw the bum out, but I just couldn't take that chance. After all, I was afraid he might actually go.

Two days passed without either of us speaking to the other, then something happened that eventually broke the ice. I don't even remember what it was now—oh yes, it was my birthday—and fairly soon things were pretty much back to normal, but with one exception. One big exception. Because I had not kicked him out, Lev now had the upper hand in our relationship. And what's worse, he knew it.

While he didn't have much control at work, Lev more than made up for it at home. He started checking my schedule, telling me when and where I could go, and with whom I could associate. I'm not just talking about my private life, but my professional one as well.

You have to understand his frustration. At the studio Lev was just another behind-the-scenes employee. But he wanted more—he wanted to be included. To rub elbows with the rich and famous. And, you see, the only entry he had into that world was through me.

So he forced his way in. Started attending parties with

me, showing up at business luncheons, coming along to negotiating sessions. Of course, that didn't last long. It was a
total disaster. The rich and famous, whose acceptance he so
craved, simply ignored him.

After a few weeks, he stopped trying. I could tell I was losing him. He was becoming more and more distant, more
and more withdrawn from the relationship. I didn't know
what to do. I was afraid our life together was coming to an
end, especially if Lev were to meet someone else.

And, strangely enough, that was exactly what happened.
Another man did come along. But things didn't go quite the
way I had feared. In fact, this man's entrance into our lives
ended up saving the relationship. Or opening Pandora's box,
depending on how you look at it.

That man was Brock Galloway. All most people remember about him now are either his romantic comedies or his
tragic death. But back then he was just unknown Homer
Watts, recently arrived in Hollywood from Sioux Falls, South
Dakota, fresh-faced and clean-cut. Another aspiring actor.
Eager. Ambitious. And probably the most free-spirited young
man I've ever met.

He virtually camped out on my office sofa. The minute
the doors opened in the morning, he was there. And he
stayed all day. He kept this up for over a week, until I finally
agreed to see him.

About the only thing he had going for him was his looks.
He had done some high school plays and not much more.
But he didn't lack confidence. He was certain he would be a

star. He just needed that lucky break, and he needed me to represent him.

I tell you, I think it was his enthusiasm that finally won me over, more than anything else. He was a big, strapping boy, just turned twenty. I told him I thought I might be able to get him work as a walk-on or an extra, but I wasn't optimistic. The years following the war had seen Hollywood flooded with thousands of beautiful hopefuls, both men and women. Guys like Homer were a dime a dozen.

And that name had to go. I told him no actor named Homer would ever have any marquee value. But he was ahead of me on that one. Had already picked out a new name, he said. Brock Galloway. I liked it, and we signed the representation contracts that afternoon.

There was just one problem. He had no phone, no residence, and no money. The entire time he had been in town, he had been sleeping in Echo Park at night, scrounging food off other people's plates at Schwab's, and living in my office during the day. He had been washing himself and his clothes in the men's room of an Esso station down the street. I couldn't think what else to do, so I took him home.

Big mistake. Lev took one look at him, and I knew I was in trouble. I don't know if Brock read the lust in Lev's eyes, but I did. I knew it was just a matter of time before Lev put the move on Brock. But I also knew he would be discreet around me.

But things didn't quite go as I had expected, or I'm sure as Lev had expected either. At that time we were still living in a small two-bedroom bungalow in the hills just above Hollywood Boulevard. Lev and I shared the big bedroom, but the other was left primarily for storage, since we never had any overnight guests. Until Brock, that is.

Well, Lev cleaned some of the junk out of the spare bedroom, and we left Brock to his own devices. We were just going to bed ourselves when Brock suddenly stormed in.

He stood in the doorway stark naked. I'll never forget his first words. "Can I join the fun?" he asked.

And he did.

Brock stayed with us for five months, during which time I managed to get him signed to a seven-year stock contract at Universal. The last week he was with us, after he had already found an apartment of his own and was in the process of furnishing it, Brock suggested that we make a permanent record of our time together. He asked Lev to film our bedroom antics.

Needless to say, I was not thrilled with the idea, but I could see immediately that Lev was. And I knew my objections would be overruled. But I still advised caution.

The next day Lev brought an eight millimeter camera home from the studio, and he set up the bedroom with lights and sound just as if he were filming a regular motion picture. First he filmed Brock by himself, then he directed me to join the action. I balked, and no amount of persuasion would get me to change my mind. Finally Lev showed me how to operate the camera, and he joined Brock on the bed.

I hated every minute of it, but Brock had awakened a new interest in Lev. One that would change our lives forever.

CHAPTER 5

"Some secrets
should remain silent,
some shame
should remain private,
some shadows
should remain dark."

—Stokes Moran,
on Edward Mathis' *Out of the Shadows*

"Well?"

It was after two in the morning when I got back to Lee's apartment. I had expected her to be asleep at this hour, but I had underestimated the depth of her insatiable curiosity. I found her waiting impatiently for my return.

"Well what?" As exhausted as I was, I was not too tired to tease.

"Well, what did Izzy want?"

"Nothing," I answered.

"Nothing?" Lee repeated incredulously. "You've been with him for almost four hours, and you expect me to believe he told you nothing."

I shrugged out of my coat, tossed it carelessly on the back of a chair, and collapsed on her living-room sofa.

"I'm tired," I said, kicking my shoes off and nudging them out of sight under the cocktail table. "Can't this wait till morning?"

"No! I want to know now!"

"Oh well, if you insist. But I'll need a cup of coffee first."

"I've already got a pot going." Lee headed toward the kitchen. "I'll just be a minute," she called.

While Lee was gone, I thought back over the last few hours and Izzy's unexpected revelations.

* * *

More than a year passed, *Izzy had continued his story*, before it happened again. But all that time, I had been waiting. Waiting for the other shoe to drop, I suppose. I knew Lev had tasted something tantalizing, something illicit, something dangerous. And that he would eventually succumb again.

If anything surprised me, it was that he let so much time elapse. But looking back, I know now Lev was just waiting for the right person.

I tried to keep my male clients away from him, not because I thought he would try to seduce them, but because I knew he could seduce me. And that was virtually the same thing.

Remember the time. It was nineteen fifty. Hollywood was the dream factory to the world. Not just the celluloid dreams created for the screen, but the very real dreams found in the aspiring hearts of thousands of young men and women who flocked to Los Angeles each year, hoping to make it big. And not much has changed over the years.

I'd say the biggest difference between then and now is the loss of innocence. Today's kids are much more cynical, much more aware of the price that must be paid, and much more likely to pay it. Back then, the kids were just starry-eyed and trusting high school Romeos and Juliets out to make their mark on the world. Then and now, Hollywood has always had a never-ending supply of vulnerable and disposable children.

But back in nineteen fifty, they weren't children merely by the dates on their birth certificates. No, they were "of age," as we used to say. They were children because of their sheltered upbringings and their lack of awareness of the harsh realities of the movie industry. Believe me, Hollywood provides a quick wake-up call to the facts of life. It's strictly a business, and its principal commodity has always been beautiful bodies.

And many of these beautiful bodies found their way to my office door. Just like Brock, their pathetic hopes and naked desires overwhelmed their common sense. But unlike Brock, most didn't have the talent to match their ambition.

I turned most of these spurious actors and actresses away. After all, I had a thriving agency and already represented many well-established clients. Why take on the aggravation of the untested, the unproven, the unskilled? I have never been a Pygmalion, never wanted to be. It just takes too much effort.

But in the back of my mind, I knew the real reason. I

knew their unchecked lust for stardom was just the opening Lev would use to get the young men into our bed, in front of our camera. He also had an unchecked lust. I had seen it come to life that afternoon with Brock. And I knew it would just be a matter of time before it repeated itself.

So eventually all of my justifications, delays, and evasions went for nothing. One September day Lev spotted Michael Bolding sitting in my outer office. Within two weeks, we had our second filmed escapade. And I had a new client.

I know this all sounds reprehensible to you. It does to me, too. In a way. I offer no excuses, no alibis. It was a simple transaction. My power for their bodies. I suppose my only defense is to remind you that seduction is a two-way street. The seducer can't succeed without a somewhat willing subject. Willing to sell their souls to a Hollywood devil.

* * *

Izzy fell silent, then abruptly got off the bed, walked to his closet, and retrieved a leather-bound album from the overhead shelf. He brought it back to me and placed it in my lap. I looked at him questioningly.

"The final tally was twenty-six," he said. "Lev and I were always careful, though, not to let any of them know that they were just one among many. As far as they knew, it was a one-time aberration for all of us. But Lev and I knew differently, and when it was done, the collection spanned a quarter of a century—from nineteen forty-nine through nineteen seventy-four. And, around number twenty-five, both Lev and I had grown tired of the game. And, I suppose, to an extent, tired of each other as well."

"What is this?" I asked, nodding toward the book on my knees.

"It's a photographic record of our filmed experiences."

My face probably registered my distress, because Izzy added, "Don't worry. It won't fall open to any embarrassing scenes."

Izzy opened the book. "See."

I looked down at an eight-by-ten color glossy, a head-and-shoulders shot of a young Brock Galloway. "Turn the page," Izzy directed.

Cautiously, I flipped the heavy lamination over and found a friendly pose of Izzy and Brock together. I thumbed through a few more pages and discovered nothing at all explicit.

"I don't understand," I admitted.

"If you'll look closely," Izzy said, "you'll see that all the pages have a zip-lock border, like a Baggie. You have to peel the edges apart to get to the pictures inside."

I nodded. That explained why the pages were so hefty, so bulky, much too thick for a normal photo album.

"Go ahead," Izzy prodded. "Where's your natural curiosity? Don't you want to see the blackmail evidence?"

I hesitated, but Izzy was right. An investigator, even an amateur one, would experience no qualms in confronting the evidence, however sordid it might be. I slipped my finger between the outer edge of one of the pages and began the separation process. While I was peeling the page apart, Izzy continued his story.

"In nineteen seventy-eight, Lev and I moved here to New York. I had purchased this brownstone back in the forties, when I was flush with money and you could still get Manhattan real estate at a fairly reasonable price. I knew one day I'd want to come back closer to my Jersey roots. Well, the late seventies was the time.

"I sold my Hollywood agency, with the exception of a few lifelong clients who insisted that I continue to represent them. So I ended up with a sort of semiretirement. And over the years, I've added an occasional client here and there. But not in show business. I was tired of Hollywood and tired of that rat race. Let Michael Ovitz and all the others rule the roost. I wanted out."

The pages now lay apart on my lap, but I kept my eyes locked on Izzy.

"So the new clients I added were all authors. After forty years in the business, I became a literary agent. And that's how I met Lee." Izzy smiled.

"I think by that time Lev and I stayed together more out of habit than anything else. We still loved each other, but I was worn out. You see, I was feeling a very old sixty-something while Lev had barely turned fifty. So I didn't mind when he started going out.

"Maybe if I had objected, things would have turned out differently. Back in those days, remember, we still didn't know about AIDS. And by the time we did, Lev already had it."

Izzy paused. I murmured an "I'm sorry." I still had not glanced down at the open page. Finally, Izzy continued.

"Lev got the full-blown disease in nineteen eighty-six, and, for some reason, he became obsessed with that old film footage of his sexual exploits. He worked night and day culling it, editing it, transferring it onto videotape. It was almost as if he saw that film as his legacy. His legacy to me, of course. Because we both agreed that it must never go beyond our eyes," Izzy stressed.

"I didn't see any harm in what Lev was doing. It certainly gave him a focus at a time when he desperately needed one.

"So, out of thousands of feet of film, Lev created a two-hour videotape. You might call it the best of the worst. Then he took certain stills from the film and made that picture album. Lev died two days after he finished the project," he concluded quietly.

Izzy sat down next to me on the sofa.

"That's Tory Andrews," he nodded toward the open book. "I think he came along about nineteen fifty-nine or sixty." I followed Izzy's gaze and finally glimpsed the revealing photos.

"All of the shots are like those," Izzy said. "For some reason, Lev chose only solo poses. Editing himself out, so to speak." Izzy stood up. "But the videotape is another matter indeed. Lev is very much in evidence in that. And that's why I must get it back. I can't let Lev down. I promised him I'd always keep it private and destroy it before I died."

The pictures had momentarily distracted me, so I thought I had missed something in Izzy's narrative.

"Get it back?" I asked. "You mean it's been stolen?"

Izzy nodded. "Because of a lonely old man's stupidity. Yes, it's been stolen."

"How?" I asked.

Izzy walked over to the window, turned his back to the glass, and looked directly at me. He started to speak, then stopped. Finally, he said, "The original films are in a safety deposit box at Chase Manhattan. But I kept the album and the videotape here. Locked away, of course, but still within easy reach. I'd occasionally play the tape, not out of any sexual need, but because of the memories. Lev is alive once again in those scenes. Strangely, that's the only living record I have of him.

"You'd think at my age I'd have learned a little discretion. But loneliness is a harsh companion.

"It was a few days after last Thanksgiving. I had gone to a publishing party at the Waldorf. Afterwards, I stopped in at the Rainbow Room for a cocktail. And I met a man.

"I don't believe he was actively cruising. The Rainbow Room is certainly not a pick-up spot, by any means. I don't know what I was thinking. I hadn't done anything like that in years. I've never been reckless, but, I don't know, he was beautiful and he bore a startling resemblance to Lev. And before I knew it, I had brought him back with me to this house.

"His name was Ted Nichols. My lifetime in show business tells me it's probably not the name he was born with. Or maybe it is. Who knows and who cares? His name wasn't important. He was young and handsome, and for a while he made me feel young and handsome again, too.

"Ted stayed with me here for almost a month. Till the day before Christmas. When he suddenly disappeared. And, as I discovered two days later, so had the videotape."

I frowned and was about to comment when Izzy hurriedly continued. "You don't have to say it. I know it was stupid to show the videotape to Ted. I just got carried away. I guess I wanted to impress him. All those famous men." Izzy laughed. "You wanna know the biggest joke? The kid didn't recognize any of them."

"Do you have any idea where this Nichols guy might be now?"

Izzy shook his head. "He told me very little about himself. He was just a two-bit hustler, and I fell for his line."

"But you think he's going to use the tape for blackmail?"

"What else would he do with it? I thought for a while he would try to ransom it back to me, but I haven't heard from him. His next most likely move is to try to extort money from the men on the tape. Wouldn't you agree?"

I nodded. "It's possible. Have you been in touch with any of those men to let them know that might happen?"

"Are you crazy?" Izzy almost shouted. "I can't talk to them about something like that. Anyway, I have no doubt I'll hear from each of them when and if Ted tries to peddle that tape."

Izzy added. "Or the few that are left, that is."

"What do you mean?" I asked.

"Of the twenty-six men on that tape, only ten are still alive."

"Are you serious?" Izzy was talking about a casualty rate that insurance companies would run from in panic.

"It was their lifestyles. Most lived too hard and too fast. Many died from AIDS. There were a couple of suicides, a few car wrecks. But mostly, I think it was Hollywood."

I frowned again. "Hollywood?"

Izzy nodded. "Hollywood uses up people fast. I'm constantly amazed I've survived this long."

I closed the album. The notion that most of those pictures were of dead men somehow upset me more than the pictures themselves. This was getting morbid in the extreme. I stood up.

"What is it you want from me, then?" I asked Izzy, perhaps a shade too abruptly.

He seemed surprised by my question. "Why, I want you to get the tape back for me. Before it does any damage."

I felt like reminding Izzy that had he really wanted to avoid that possibility, he would have destroyed that tape long ago. But recrimination could serve no useful purpose now.

"I need to know all you can tell me about this Ted Nichols."

Izzy shook his head. "I really can't tell you that much. I don't know where he lives, or where he came from. I don't even know if that's his real name."

"But there must be something you can tell me about him." I was beginning to lose my patience. "Anything at all."

"He said he was nineteen. But I think he was probably more like twenty-three. As I said, he reminded me of Lev. Light brown hair, green eyes." Izzy walked over to the bedside table and lifted a framed photograph off the top. He brought it back and handed it to me.

"That's Lev," he said.

I looked down at a boy in an army uniform. Fresh-faced, bright-eyed. The whole world ahead of him.

"Ted's not exactly a dead ringer for Lev, but there's a close enough resemblance to be recognizable. I'm afraid that's the best I can do."

I nodded. "I'll see what I can do. But you'll have to trust me to handle this in my own way." What was I saying? Did I think I would actually pursue this insanity?

"You do whatever you think best. You can keep Lev's picture and the album if you think they will help you. Oh, by the way," Izzy lifted the album from my grasp and opened it up, "the agency information on all of these men is at the back of the book. Last known addresses and so forth. If you feel you have to contact them, I won't object. It's just something I couldn't do myself."

No wonder, I thought. "I understand," I said. "But how will I know which ones are alive and which ones are . . . "

Izzy's hyenalike laugh returned. "That's easy. Look at the pictures. The dead ones have the black borders."

* * *

"So where's the album?" Lee demanded, when I had finished the story, giving her an almost verbatim account of Izzy's narrative.

"It's over there by the door, wrapped in that newspaper," I said. "I left it on the table because I didn't want you wondering what it was until I'd had a chance to fill you in."

"Well, I can't wait to see it," she said, between spoonfuls of strawberry yogurt.

"Will you do me a favor, and let it go until tomorrow?"

"Well," she said, nestling back against the sofa, "I suppose, if it'll make you happy."

"It will."

Lee laughed. "This little collection of Izzy's gives Hollywood beefcake a whole new meaning."

"Lee!" I protested. "I can't believe you're being so blasé about this. If it had been women Izzy had coerced into making these films, you'd have been outraged. I thought you'd be shocked by his revelations."

She shook her head. "I've known for years that Izzy was gay; I just never let him know I knew. And the existence of these films doesn't come as any great surprise. Just about everybody has secret vices of some kind. So it's no big deal."

"No big deal?" I mimicked. "Don't you think what Izzy did was a kind of rape?"

"No, I don't. For one thing," she explained, "from the way you've described it, no force was ever used. And, believe me, each man knew exactly what he was doing. And everybody got what they wanted out of it. It's the classic Hollywood casting couch, with the men on their backsides for a change. I think it's a kind of poetic justice."

"I can't believe I'm hearing you right." I shook my head. "And Izzy was so concerned about your feelings."

Lee smiled. "Izzy's a gentleman. He comes from the old school. Something like this is an embarrassment to him. Something he couldn't share with a woman, especially one he likes and admires. Like me."

I reminded myself that it was Lee's nonjudgmental attitude that had so attracted me to her in the first place. But I was finding her casual acceptance of Izzy's exploitive behavior a little hard to take. Especially at three in the morning.

"Why don't we save the rest of this conversation until after we've had some sleep," I suggested.

Lee nodded. "Good idea," she said, as she scraped the bottom of the yogurt cup. "We need to rest up for tomorrow anyway."

"Tomorrow?" I asked, somewhat suspiciously. "What happens tomorrow?"

"Tomorrow," Lee repeated, as she took my hand and led me toward her bedroom, "we're going after Izzy's boy toy."

CHAPTER 6

*"Finding
the insidious blackmailer
proves to be
no easy task for the
novice detective."*

—Stokes Moran,
on Kate Charles' *A Drink of Deadly Wine*

"You wouldn't believe the schoolgirl crush I had on this guy."

Lee propped Izzy's album up against the sugar, salt, and pepper containers on the kitchen table and cleared the space in front of it for her mammoth breakfast. How such a tiny woman could continue to pack away so much food constantly amazed me. This morning her menu consisted of eggs, waffles, bacon, hashed brown potatoes, toast, and coffee. My meager cup of coffee, glass of orange juice, and bowl of Grape-Nuts hugged the slender remaining strip of tabletop.

"When I was in junior high, I thought Tory Andrews was the best-looking thing in pants I'd ever seen," Lee said. "And if I'd known what he was hiding in those pants, I'd have camped out on his doorstep and gladly given him my virginity."

"Lee!" I pretended outrage.

"Oh, don't worry, lover boy," her eyes twinkled at me, "he's got nothing on you."

"That's not what I meant," I said, as I swiped a piece of Lee's buttered toast.

"I know." Lee puffed out her lips. "You think I'm being a naughty girl looking at these pictures."

"You're not just looking at them," I responded, "you're ogling them."

She laughed. "And I suppose men don't ogle *Playboy* or *Penthouse*."

"It's not the same thing," I objected.

"Why isn't it?"

"Well . . . " I hesitated, struggling to find the correct justification. "It's just not, that's all."

Lee laughed again. "Try using that argument at the Supreme Court. Or, for that matter, the Supreme Deli on Seventy-ninth Street. You'd get plastered with pastry."

"Maybe I can't put it into words," I persisted, "but I know it makes me uncomfortable."

"What does? The pictures, or my looking at them?"

"I suppose it's the pictures themselves that bother me. These men never expected to be porno pinups." I stole a slice of Lee's bacon. It broke apart as I folded it into my mouth.

"No, but they made the films." I started to object, but Lee preempted me. "It doesn't matter why they did it," Lee reiterated her point from last night. "They were all over eighteen, and they all knew perfectly well what they were doing. If they didn't want to do it, they could have said no."

"Oh sure," I scoffed. "And see their careers go right down the toilet."

Lee piled a mountain of strawberry jam on a piece of toast and waved it in my face. "Kyle, you've met Izzy. He may not be Polly Pureheart, but he is a professional."

"You call this professional." I slapped at the album, and it fell forward into Lee's plate of eggs.

"Now look what you've done."

"The pictures are protected," I said, as she wiped furiously at the vinyl cover. "Which is more than I can say for the men in them."

"I don't think we're getting anywhere. It's obvious you and I don't agree on this issue. So I suggest we just agree to disagree and move on."

I nodded. "That sounds like a good idea to me."

"What we need to be doing," Lee continued, "is tracking down Ted Nichols."

"Okay, so just how do you suggest we do that?" I asked.

"Well, for starters, I can check to see if he's listed in either Actors Equity or the Screen Actors Guild."

"You think he's an actor?"

"If Izzy is right that Ted Nichols is not his real name, maybe he changed it for the stage," Lee suggested.

I nodded approval. "Makes sense to me. And you can check that out while I head on home. Nolan didn't expect to get stuck with Bootsie the entire night. I need to take her off his hands."

"But you're not going to leave all this in my lap, are you?"

"No, you let me know what you come up with, and we'll figure out where we go from there," I said.

"And what if I come up with nothing?"

"Then I guess we follow the only other lead we have."

"And what might that be?" Lee asked.

I smiled. "Why, the pictures, of course."

* * *

Nolan was not at all upset with my tardy return. From the lewd glint in his eyes, I could tell he thought the course of true romance was running quite smoothly. If only he knew the real story. But I had promised Izzy I'd be discreet, so I left Nolan content with his correct but incomplete assumption.

I entered the house through the patio door, leaving Bootsie at play in the backyard. The kitchen was still pristine from the maid's weekly Tuesday visits, but the litter in the living room was just as I had left it yesterday afternoon. Boxes on the floor, books on the table, envelopes scattered here and there. I retrieved my luggage from the downstairs closet and carried the bags upstairs. I then went back downstairs to tackle the mess I'd left there.

For the next two hours I put things in order. I may not be a cleanness freak, but I do like tidiness. I don't function well amid chaos. So what am I doing marrying someone like Lee, I asked myself. She absolutely thrives on it.

The phone rang.

"I struck out," Lee said, without preamble. "I also

checked with NYPD to see if they had any priors on Ted Nichols. Nothing." I could hear the frustration in her voice. "Any suggestions?"

"Izzy may be right that Nichols' first inclination would be toward blackmail," I said. "But . . . "

"But what?"

"I wouldn't be so sure he wouldn't try to peddle the tape to someplace like the *National Enquirer* or *Hustler*."

"It would certainly be quicker," Lee agreed.

"And less complicated," I added.

"Let me make some more calls. I'm pretty sure I can find out if anyone's offering something this sensational for sale."

"Good girl," I said, and then regretted my choice of words. But Lee did not take offense at my sexist slip.

"I'll get back to you," is all she said as she severed the connection.

I placed the receiver back on its holder, walked upstairs, and entered my bedroom. Earlier I had deposited my suitcases on the bed. Now it was time to unpack, something I always hated to do.

Make it simple, I tempted myself, just throw everything in the washer. But I really couldn't do that. Certain things don't mix too well with soap and water. Like my electric razor, my blow-dryer, and my manuscript.

My manuscript. I had forgotten I had stashed it away in the bottom of one of my bags. I lifted the fifty-some typewritten sheets from their nesting place, survived the momentary desire to chuck them in the garbage, and instead carried them over to the window seat. I sat down and started reading the first lines.

Before I knew it, I had read through the entire thing. It was better than I had remembered. Almost two weeks had passed since I had last worked on my mystery novel. Maybe the time away from it had given me a new perspective.

I moved over to my computer terminal, plugged in the machinery, loaded the document file, scrolled to the last page, and began to write. Strangely, despite the layoff, the story flowed rather smoothly from my head onto the monitor's screen. It was almost as if I had not missed a beat since the last time I had worked on it.

The phone rang. Damn, I said to myself, just when I'm getting started. But as I lifted my bedside phone from its cradle, my eyes caught the digital readout on my clock radio. More than five hours had passed since I had come upstairs to unpack.

"Kyle," it was Lee. "Are you there? Say something."

"Oh." Temporarily disoriented, I hastily recovered. "Yes, Lee, I'm here."

"Well, you didn't say anything."

"I was working on my novel. And guess what?" I could hear the excitement in my voice. "It's not as bad as I remembered."

"Of course it's not," Lee said matter-of-factly. "I told you that."

"It had seemed pretty awful to me."

"You were just being too hard on yourself. After all, this is your first try. It's not like writing a review. You can't expect it to be as easy as that. Writing a novel is hard work, something you're not used to." Was that a dig? Or a compliment? I couldn't tell. Lee continued, "All you needed was a little breather. Now you see it more objectively. The way I see it."

I wasn't sure I agreed with her last statement. As the past few days had clearly demonstrated, Lee and I seldom see eye to eye on anything. Like Izzy Cohen, for instance. Which prompted me to ask, "Did you come up with anything?"

"No." I could hear the frustration in her voice. "I talked to half a dozen people. If that videotape is up for grabs, none of the obvious people knows anything about it. And these people make it their business to know something like that."

I heard a scratch downstairs at the back door. Bootsie was signaling that she wanted in. Either she was tired, or hungry, or lonely. Or all three. But she would just have to wait. Lee and I had a problem to solve first.

"What do you suggest now?" I asked.

"Me? These were my best ideas, and they've gotten us nowhere. I think it's your turn to come up with something brilliant."

I tried to recall the techniques Lew Archer or Kinsey Millhone employed to track down someone who didn't want to be found. Their next step always seemed so logical, so practical, the kind of thing the reader shakes his head over and ruminates, "Why didn't I think of that?" Well, right now, why couldn't I think of something?

And I did. Where the idea came from I'll never know. Maybe Lew or Kinsey sent it to me by way of inspiration.

"Why don't we put an ad in the newspaper," I suggested.

"What do you mean?"

"We could make a direct appeal to Ted Nichols. In the *Times*. No, scratch that; he's not likely to read the *Times*. In the *Daily News*. Yes, that's it."

I was warming up to the idea. And so was Lee.

"You're saying that instead of us finding him, we should get him to find us?" I could still hear skepticism in her voice. But now it was laced with a kinetic excitement as well.

"Yes, that's it exactly," I answered immediately.

"Okay, genius, so just how do we accomplish that?" she asked.

"By making the ad as mysterious, as compelling, as we possibly can."

"Like what?"

I thought for a minute. "Like 'Ted Nichols. You have the tape. We have the money. Call 455-7377.' "

Lee laughed. "I don't think so." She paused. I waited. Finally, she said, "You know, it just might work. Crazy as it sounds, it just might work. But I'm sure we can come up with a better-worded enticement."

In the end, Lee and I settled on a much simpler wording. When it ran two days later, the ad read merely 'Ted Nichols. Important. Please call 203-555-8080.' Since Lee's phone gets so much business use, we decided to list my number instead. The ad ran for a week. Not only in the *Daily News*, but in *Newsday* as well. But with no response by the seventh and final day, Lee and I were both ready to admit defeat.

"It was worth a try," Lee said. She had arrived at my house a couple of hours before, and we had just finished lunch. Pizza and salad, which Lee had graciously picked up at The Ultimate Experience Pizza Parlor on her way into Tipton. Carrying our coffee cups with us, we moved into the more comfortable surroundings of the living room when Lee made her generous pronouncement.

"You're just saying that to make me feel better," I protested. Not wanting to be left out, Bootsie pushed her way in between the couch and the cocktail table, turned her usual three times, and plopped down at my feet, her nose resting easily on the top of my shoe.

"No I'm not," Lee responded. "I still think it was a good idea. It's just that nothing came of it, that's all."

"My first time up at bat as a detective and I strike out."

"Don't take it so hard." Lee smiled, and her white teeth flashed. "Not even Travis McGee got it right every time."

"I was thinking more of Lew Archer." We both laughed. Just then, the phone rang. I automatically reached to pick it up.

"Hello," I said.

The masculine voice on the other end of the line said, "I'm calling about your ad in the newspaper."

My tongue felt bloated, heavy. "Yes?" I croaked. I waved excitedly at Lee. "What can I do for you?" I added.

"That's what I'd like to know," he answered. "I'm Ted Nichols."

CHAPTER 7

*"It's not the plot
that matters so much;
it's the fun
the reader has along the way."*

—Stokes Moran,
on Mickey Friedman's *A Temporary Ghost*

$\mathcal{B}$ut it was the wrong Ted Nichols.

The caller turned out to be a thirty-eight-year-old investment banker from Stamford. A nice guy, a little irritated that he'd made the telephone call for nothing. I promised him my business the next time I needed financial advice.

Lee and I gave the ad another two days, but sham Ted was the only nibble we got. Finally, two weeks to the day since Izzy had saddled me with this problem, I called Lee at her Manhattan apartment.

"It's time to try something else," I said. "The newspaper idea just didn't pan out."

I guess she heard the discouragement in my voice, because she said, "It was still worth a try."

"Yeah," I answered. "Just like the phone book in New Orleans." I stopped, remembering we had once again overlooked the obvious. "Hey," I started, but Lee cut me off.

"I already checked," she said. "No Ted Nichols listed in any directory anywhere in the New York area. And only one Theodore. But a ton of Nichols, too many for us to try and cover."

"Well, it was still worth a try," I mimicked.

"Thanks a lot." Lee laughed. "I even went down to the New York Public Library and checked through the L.A. phone directories. Nothing there either."

"So what now? We go after the men in the album?" I asked.

"That's what I've been thinking for the past week," Lee answered. "I spoke to Izzy three days ago . . . "

"Three days ago? You didn't have much faith in my idea, did you?"

"When there was no response to the ad right away, I just felt it wasn't going to work." Lee's matter-of-fact voice gave lie to her earlier "it was still worth a try" sentiment.

"Anyway, I decided it was time for me to talk to Izzy myself," she continued. "I didn't want him thinking anything had changed between him and me."

"Well, had it?"

"He seemed a little bit awkward at first. As I said before, there are some things Izzy will never feel comfortable talking to a woman about."

"So how did you deal with it?"

"Basically, we talked around it. I told him we weren't getting anywhere tracking Ted Nichols down, that I thought the only viable alternative left to us was to contact the men in the photos."

I could just picture Izzy's reaction to that suggestion, so I said as much to Lee.

"Not at all," Lee protested. "In fact, Izzy said if that's what we thought best, he wouldn't interfere. We could do whatever we felt was necessary."

"He must be pretty desperate," I said.

"He is," Lee said. "He didn't say so, but I think he has two primary concerns. One, of course, is that Ted Nichols does no damage."

"Yes," I agreed. "He said as much to me."

"And two, I think he misses the tape. All those years, all those memories."

"All that Lev," I added, remembering Izzy's words.

"Exactly."

"So what next?" I asked.

"I've booked us on a flight to Los Angeles. We leave to-morrow morning at ten."

"Hey, just a minute, where's the money coming from?"

"Oh, didn't I tell you?" Lee asked innocently. "To cover any expenses we might incur, Izzy gave me a check for ten thousand dollars."

* * *

I held in my lap an advance reading copy of the new Eliza-beth George, but I was merely staring at the words, not reg-istering their meaning at all. No reflection on Lynley and

Travers, they're usually very good airplane company. It's just that my mind kept wandering.

Six of the ten surviving members of Izzy's little video club apparently still lived in the Southern California area, according to agency records. Two others didn't even live in the United States any longer—the first had purchased his own little Bali Hai somewhere in the South Pacific and now ruled the place like a king in exile, and the second had gone looking for his own personal guru back in the sixties and had remained somewhere high in the Himalayas ever since. Lee and I had agreed to scratch both of those names off our list entirely—if we'd have trouble reaching them, we argued, so would Ted Nichols—he'd go after the easier targets, as would we. That left us with eight active possibilities, the last two men on Izzie's list having returned to their original hometowns—one in Pennsylvania, the other in Vermont. Those we would get to eventually, but, rejecting geographic proximity, Lee and I had decided to go first for the Hollywood half-dozen.

Again, it was Lee's persuasiveness that had swayed the debate. "Ted Nichols has the tape," she had argued, "we have the album. But we also have something he doesn't have. Names and addresses. All Nichols knows is what Izzy told him—namely, that these men, at least in their heyday, had been Hollywood stars. So, with nothing else to go on, doesn't it make sense that Nichols would head for L.A.?"

I eventually capitulated to her argument. Not that I for a

minute doubted her logic, I just didn't want another trip. Leaving home, boarding Bootsie at Dr. Nancy's animal clinic, packing and unpacking, asking Nolan to gather my mail, enduring restaurant food, sleeping in strange beds. It just wasn't worth the bother.

But both Lee and I had agreed that this was too delicate a matter to entrust to the telephone. You just don't call up a stranger, remind him of an embarrassing episode from his past, and inquire if he's being blackmailed over it. No telling the kind of responses we'd get with that approach. We still weren't sure how we were going to handle it in person, only that face-to-face was the better way.

Also, we felt Ted Nichols wouldn't attempt long-distance blackmail himself. For one thing, he'd have to convince his victims he had the evidence, and he could hardly do that over the phone. Then, if he succeeded in hooking a sucker, he'd need to be there for the payoff. He wouldn't want to be three thousand miles away.

If blackmail were the motive, that is, and I was still not convinced that it was. Surely if these men had already been contacted by Ted Nichols, they would have immediately screamed bloody murder at Izzy. For his incompetence, if for nothing else. But thus far, not a peep out of any of them.

My doubts notwithstanding, Lee and I now found our-selves in two first-class seats on a United flight out of JFK. Scheduled to arrive in Los Angeles at twelve fifty P.M., Pacific Standard Time.

* * *

"*Farewell, My Lovely.*"

"What?" Lee startled awake. "Are we there? Have we landed?" Lee reached under her seat for her purse.

"No, no, no," I reassured her. "We're still in the air. Somewhere over Kansas, I suspect. Just settle down and go back to sleep."

"But I know I heard you say good-bye to somebody. You're not planning on jumping out of the plane, are you?" Lee smiled.

"I must have spoken aloud, without realizing it." I then explained to her about the mystery anthology and the editor's request for my ten all-time favorite mystery novels. For the past few minutes, I had been lost in an internal debate over whether to list Raymond Chandler's *The Lady in the Lake* or *Farewell, My Lovely*. I had finally decided on the latter.

"And must have done so too emphatically," I concluded.

"How far have you gotten?" Lee asked.

"Just two," I said. "It's been more difficult than I imagined."

Lee stretched, refluffed her pillow, and rearranged it behind her head. "Besides *Farewell, My Lovely*, what have you settled on?"

"Agatha Christie's *Curtain*," I said.

"No!" Lee rocked forward in her seat, the pillow slipping down behind her. "Why not *The Murder of Roger Ackroyd* or *The ABC Murders*?"

"I considered those Christies, and several others. But I finally opted for the death of Poirot."

Lee retrieved her pillow and repositioned it around her shoulders. "But surely it can't be your favorite Christie. There are at least a dozen that are better."

"Well, it's my choice, and I'm sticking with it," I said. "You think we could find something else to argue over instead of *Curtain*."

"I'm not so sure," Lee said absently.

"What do you mean by that?" If she wanted a fight, I was ready to give her one.

"Oh, nothing." Her voice was flat, noncommittal. "I'm thinking."

Just like a woman, I thought. Starts something, stirs up a man, and then leaves him hanging. I was poised for combat, with no opponent in the arena. Suddenly, Lee sprang to life.

"I love it," she said.

"Love what?" I asked, frustrated.

"Forget the anthology," Lee announced. "And send your regrets to the editor."

"I don't want to forget anything," I responded irritably. "And I'm not going to send anybody my regrets. I want to do this."

"Of course you do," Lee said. "And you will. But not for him."

"You've lost me." I was just about ready to toss her out the emergency exit, without a parachute.

Lee turned to me, excitement in her eyes. "You do your

own book. The more I think about it, the more certain I am."

"Certain of what?" Normally Lee made more sense. "I can't do a whole book around my ten favorite mysteries."

"No, of course not," Lee agreed. "But that will be one element. And maybe your ten favorite mystery movies as well. And some other interesting tidbits you can throw in."

"You're talking nonsense," I said, still lost as to where Lee was heading. "No company would publish something like that, and no reader would buy it. I can tell you that."

"Of course they wouldn't. You don't understand," Lee said.

"Well, why don't you enlighten me?"

"We can call it *Murderous Intentions*. Or maybe *Weighing the Evidence*. Or better yet, *Alias Stokes Moran*. Yes, I think I like the last one best."

This insanity had gone on long enough. "What are you talking about?" I demanded.

Lee turned back to me, the fire still in her eyes. "A book of your best reviews. Maybe a hundred of them. Interspersed with your lists of favorite books, movies. Maybe even broken down into subcategories, like your favorite Christmas mysteries, or favorite ecclesiastical mysteries."

"Favorite first mysteries." I joined the bandwagon.

"Yes, now you're getting it."

"I could even include some strange top-tens."

"Like what?"

"You know," I explained, "ten worst mysteries, ten weird-est titles, stuff like that."

"That's great," Lee agreed. "Kind of like a takeoff on David Letterman."

"More like a takeoff on Stokes Moran," I corrected.

Lee straightened in her seat and closed her eyes. "I'm sure I can sell the concept to a publisher. I'll send a fax out-lining my proposal to a couple of editors as soon as we get to our hotel."

"Don't you think this can wait until we get back to New York?"

Lee's eyes popped open, and she turned once again toward me. "Not on your life. It's already mid-January. This needs to be a Christmas book, so we don't have any time to lose."

"This Christmas?" I was dumbfounded.

"Don't be so skeptical. You won't have to do much at all. Just pick your best reviews. They're already written. And add a little lagniappe to the mix with those top-ten lists."

"We'd need some artwork," I mentioned.

"We could include authors' photos," Lee offered. "They'd love the publicity."

"Or dust jackets that have my words on them," I sug-gested.

"That's an idea," Lee said. "How many are there?"

"If you include both hardcover and paperback editions," I reflected, "I suppose more than a hundred."

"Wonderful. People love illustrations. And I'm sure the

publishers would be happy to grant reprint permission. That way we could make it a coffee-table book. One with a hefty price tag."

I was still stunned at the suddenness with which the book had taken shape.

"You really think people will go for it?" I asked.

"Sure," Lee said. "And the great thing about it is that it'll be so easy. It's almost a ready-made book."

"I don't know," I cautioned. "It seems a little bit manufactured to me. It doesn't quite seem honest somehow. Just throwing together odds and ends. It sounds like a rip-off."

Lee stared at me. "A rip-off?" she repeated derisively. "What do you think publishing is anyway? Do you suppose for a minute that the Madonna book was intended as a literary enterprise? Not on your life. Publishing is first and foremost a business. The men and women who run it might aspire to a higher plane, but the bottom line is always the bottom line. Making money."

I was appalled. "That's an awfully cynical point of view," I said.

"It's a cynical business."

I recalled other publishing events that had made national headlines during my lifetime—the Howard Hughes hoax, the Hitler diaries. "I guess you're right," I conceded.

"I know I'm right," Lee said, clasping her hands on top of her head. "And there's one other thing you're overlooking."

"What's that?" I asked.

"Having one book already in print will just make it that much easier for me to sell your novel when the time comes." She then added an exclamation point to her meaning. "A helluva lot easier!"

I decided to defer to Lee's experience. She was the expert in this area; she knew what the industry and the public would buy. But I attempted one last salvo anyway.

"You're sure they'd go for something like this?" I asked.

"Of course," Lee barked, then realizing her harsh tone, added more calmly, "you're one of the leading mystery critics in America. I think it's past time that you put out a book like this. Aren't you proud of your reviews? Don't you think they're worth something?"

I nodded agreement.

"You're a mystery lover," she continued. "You'll be giving other mystery lovers what they want, something they couldn't get anywhere else. You'll be giving good value."

"All right." I accepted all her arguments. "When do we start?"

"Right now," she replied firmly. "Keep working on your top-ten list. And start compiling the reviews. And the other lists. In my fax, I'll offer the finished book by the first of the month."

"What?" I was astounded. "By the first of February. That's impossible!"

"No it's not. We've got to move fast on this. And believe me, if we want to get this book on some publisher's Christmas list, we can't waste any time."

"But we've got this job to do for Izzy," I protested.

"No problem," Lee said. "The two shouldn't interfere with each other. We can do both."

Both? I had serious doubts we could do either. But then, what did I know?

CHAPTER 8

*"When not
preoccupied with sleuthing,
the couple
has a grand time
exchanging mindless banter."*

—Stokes Moran,
on Ron Goulart's
Now He Thinks He's Dead

$\mathcal{L}$os Angeles. City of the Angels. It had been fifteen years since I had last set foot in L.A., marking the end of my self-imposed five-year sojourn in the fun-and-sun capital of the Western Hemisphere. Now I was back, and I couldn't believe how much the place had changed.

Gone was the take-it-easy, kick-your-shoes-off, ain't-life-grand lazy ennui. The smugly superior aren't-we-glad-we're-not-New-York-or-Chicago mentality. The thumb-your-nose-at-all-collars-and-ties attitude.

Los Angeles had joined the rat race.

What had been a loosely connected string of transplanted Midwestern towns masquerading as a cosmopolitan unit had transmogrified into a megalomaniacal metropolis. Los

Angeles had lost the L.A. flavor, the L.A. buzz. The city had become just another carbon-copy urban American nightmare. Rush, build, burn. I hated it.

Of course, I formed these lasting impressions during Lee's forty-five minute maneuver through the perilous minefields of L.A. traffic. Maybe I was being too hasty in my judgment, too eager to embrace the past, too willing to reject the present. Still, the city was not at all as I remembered it.

"Don't let it get you down," Lee comforted, as she took a right turn off Wilshire. "Don't forget, it's not just L.A. that's changed. There's also a world of difference between a boy of twenty-five and a man of forty. The city's not the same because you're not the same."

Yes, but this was my town. Like New York was hers. Even though Lee had been to L.A. for occasional visits over the years, she had never really gotten to know the city, and I had planned to show her all the landmarks, all my old haunts, all the special memories.

Right from the beginning, I made a mistake. As Lee braked the maroon Cadillac Seville to a stop at the car-rental exit, I insisted that she stay off the freeways and stick with the surface streets. I then directed her down Olympic, up Robertson, across to Wilshire. What I had envisioned as Lee's basic L.A. indoctrination turned instead into my unexpected and unwanted education.

Change should be sipped slowly, like a martini. The Angelenos who had lived here for the last decade and a half probably had no difficulty accepting the gradual evolution of their city. But for me, the difference was all too sudden, too jarring, too sad.

And, worst of all, the hat was gone.

If my memory of the city's former geography was at all trustworthy, the Brown Derby no longer occupied its former location on Wilshire. Lee remarked that she thought she had heard that it had been moved intact to the top of some shopping center. But I was not appeased. If this were indeed the right location, where once that proud fedora had commanded rapt respect there now sprawled a modern strip mall. Or maybe the site had been another block down where a new high rise stood, cold and pristine in its anonymity. Which opened my eyes to another unexpected phenomenon.

Los Angeles had a skyline. And a very impressive one, at that. Believe me, it came as quite a shock, something akin to a protective father suddenly realizing that his teenage daughter has sprouted a bosom.

What in the mid-seventies had been the occasional skinny toothpick sticking into the heavens had by the nineties multiplied into skyscraper mania.

By the time Lee aimed the Cadillac into the parking entrance of the Bonaventure Hotel, I was ready to get back on the plane and head home. Back to Bootsie, back to my quiet cul-de-sac, back to sanity and reason, back to a world that didn't slap me down with cruel surprise.

"Here we are," Lee announced as she killed the engine and withdrew the key from the ignition.

"Whoop-de-do," I said.

"Kyle, everything will be fine." Lee reached over and patted my hand. "You'll see."

"Yeah," I muttered, as I reached for the door handle. "That's exactly what I'm afraid of."

* * *

"Who do we try first?" I asked, as the bellman closed the door behind him.

"Slow down," Lee said, as she collapsed on the king-size bed. "Let's get unpacked before we start Sherman's march to the sea."

"I don't want to unpack," I said belligerently. "I want to get this thing over and done with."

"We've got six men to see," Lee reminded me. "That's going to take time."

"Why?" I walked to the window and looked out over the city. The glass skyscrapers gleamed in the early afternoon sunshine. I spotted the Bank of America towers, the First Interstate Bank (formerly United California Bank), and One Wilshire, where I had worked for a year and a half when I first came to L.A. Lee joined me at the window.

"Kyle, things change. People change." She slipped her hand in mine and gave a light squeeze. "Don't let it bother you so much."

I nodded absently, squeezing her hand to let her know I understood. And just what about the people, I wondered. I had thought I'd contact some of my old friends while I was here. Now I wasn't so sure I wanted to. If the city had altered so greatly in fifteen years, what metamorphosis would I find in the familiar faces? Or they in me? I decided I didn't want to know.

I turned abruptly from the window. "Let's get unpacked," I said. "We've got a lot of ground to cover. It's time we got started."

"First things first." Lee placed her portable fax machine on the top of the writing desk. "Right now I'm going to fax your book proposal to a publisher friend of mine. If we want to get the book in the fall catalogue, I've decided to offer him an exclusive. Maybe that'll increase his interest and speed things up as well." She winked at me. "Who knows? Something constructive might come out of this trip yet."

* * *

Two hours later, after getting our belongings stowed away and following a late room-service lunch in our room, we finally got down to business.

"According to Izzy's notes," Lee said, flattening the map of the Southland against the surface of the writing table, "two of the guys live in West L.A., one in Malibu, one in Long Beach, one in Pasadena, and one in Sherman Oaks."

"There used to be a mystery bookstore in Sherman Oaks," I noted matter-of-factly. "I wonder if it's still there."

"I don't know and I don't care," Lee answered. "Forget about shopping on this trip. We have a job to do."

"So, do you have any idea how we go about doing it?"

Lee looked up from the map. "I met with Izzy again yesterday," she said.

"What!" I exclaimed in surprise. "Why didn't you tell me?"

"I'm telling you now. And," she continued before I could interrupt, "he gave me a whole pile of notes on the men we'd be meeting, and he also told me how we could approach the men without interference."

Lee pushed back her chair, walked over to the closet, pulled out her satchel, and brought it back to the table. She opened the catch, turned the satchel upside down, and emptied the contents onto the tabletop. Six brightly wrapped packages tumbled out.

"What are those?" I asked.

"Mementos. Keepsakes. Presents from Izzy." Then Lee added, somewhat smugly, "and our way in."

"I don't understand," I said.

"The main problem we face," Lee said as she reclaimed her chair, "is to get the men to talk to us. We're strangers to them. If we mention the tape right away, they may take us for blackmailers. And shut us out even before we have a chance to explain, especially if Ted Nichols hasn't contacted them. Izzy feels, and I agree, that they'd be much more inclined to meet with us if we had some sort of enticement to offer them."

"I see," I said. "Do you know what's in those packages?"

Lee shook her head. "All Izzy said was they were items that would have special significance to the six men. Things personal to them and to Izzy, I should think."

"For all you know, we could be running drugs." But I said it with a smile.

"Izzy wouldn't do that to us." Lee smiled back. "But you'd better believe I'm dying of curiosity."

"Well, then, why don't we open the packages and find out?" I reached for one, but Lee intercepted my hand.

"Kyle, this whole job is a matter of trust. Between Izzy and us. Between Izzy and these men. We can't violate that trust."

I stood up. "Okay," I said. "I assume it goes something like this. We call a guy up, tell him we're friends of Izzy's, that we've got something Izzy asked us to deliver, and could we meet with him. Is that pretty much it?"

"Right," Lee answered.

"So, who's first on the list?"

"It's up to you."

"Let's hit West L.A. first. It's probably the closest, and maybe if we're lucky, we can get two out of the way tonight."

Lee looked down at Izzy's notes, found the addresses, then located them on the map.

"Mickey Allen, now Mike Conover, lives on King's Road, just south of Sunset, a little east of La Cienega. And," she paused while she zeroed in on the next location, "Cash Hardesty lives between Sunset and Hollywood, on Alta Vista, just west of La Brea." Lee looked up. "So which one do you want to try first?"

"Call them both," I said. "Let them decide."

* * *

Mickey Allen, aka Mike Conover, got the kewpie doll. He told Lee he wasn't working today and that he would be delighted for us to come right on over. Cash Hardesty wasn't quite so forthcoming but agreed to see us at seven P.M. Since I supposedly knew my way around L.A., I drove. Lee filled me in on Mickey Allen during the twenty-five minute trip.

"His full name is Michael Allen Conover," she said, paraphrasing Izzy's notes. "The producers of his sixties sitcom shortened his name to Mickey Allen. He played the middle son on 'The Bugle Boys.' The show ran for four years and is now seen in syndication in two hundred and thirty-three markets worldwide."

"Wait a minute," I said, braking for a stoplight. "A kid star is in Izzy's collection?"

"Yeah," she said, picking up the album and flipping to the back. "But Izzy made a point of noting that Mike had turned eighteen by the time they got together. In fact, Mike was the very last one. In nineteen seventy-four. Here he is." She held the full-face photo up for me to see.

The light changed to green, and I pressed the accelerator, perhaps a little too hard. The Cadillac's tires screeched.

"Kyle!" Lee cautioned.

"Sorry," I said. "I didn't mean to. It's just he seems awfully young."

"According to Izzy," Lee again looked at the notes, "he and Lev had not intended to add Mike to the collection.

They had gone three years, thought they were done with it, really didn't want to do another. But he says Mike kinda forced the issue."

"Yeah, sure," I commented skeptically. "How could an eighteen-year-old kid force two adults into anything?"

"No, that's what Izzy says. Here, let me read you exactly what he's written." Lee then gave voice to the words on the page. "When Mickey's series ended in nineteen seventy, I had trouble placing him in anything but a few commercials. Like most child actors, he had reached that awkward in-between stage where he was no longer a cute kid and was not yet ready for adult parts. He got into trouble. At sixteen, he was arrested on a drug charge. He didn't have to serve any time but he was placed on probation.

"I didn't hear from him for a couple of years after that. Then one day he just showed up on my doorstep. Said he didn't have anywhere else to go. I called his father who told me in no uncertain terms that he had washed his hands of the boy and had kicked him out of the house four months earlier. His father let me know quite succinctly that he didn't care what happened to the boy.

"I let Mike, as he now called himself, stay with Lev and me for a few days until I could figure out what to do with him. It was during one of those days, while Lev and I were out shopping, that Mike rifled the house and found the films. Not all of them, mind you, just three or four. Lev had the films hidden in various parts of the house, so that if someone ever did break in, they wouldn't get the whole lot.

"So, that afternoon when we got back from the grocery store, Lev and I found Mike watching one of the films. He had carted all the equipment out of the closet, threaded the projector, and set up the screen. Calm as you please. Like he owned the place.

"Needless to say, I was furious. I ordered Mike out of my house, but my tirade had no effect on him. He merely said either we filmed him, or he'd turn us in to the police.

"I told him to go ahead, that we'd handle whatever came down. He asked, even a drug charge? and then told us he had hidden a bag of Quaaludes somewhere in the house, and did we want to see who could find it first—us or the cops?

"Lev and I decided not to risk it. So Mike, at the ripe old age of eighteen, became the youngest, and last, member of our little group."

"Damn," I said, when Lee had finished the reading, "this Mickey Allen—"

"Mike Conover," she corrected.

"Mike Conover," I repeated grudgingly. "But no matter what his name is, he sounds like a real piece of work."

As it turned out, he was.

CHAPTER 9

*"Wise readers
would be well advised
to add
this author's criminous ABC's
to their basic
mystery education."*

—Stokes Moran,
on Sue Grafton's *"H" Is for Homicide*

"Blackmail? You've got to be kidding!" Then he laughed.

Mike Conover's response to our news was hardly what Lee and I expected. But then, the entire experience had not been exactly as we had anticipated.

We had located his address without too much difficulty. Conover lived in an upscale section of the city, on a slightly sloping hill, in a converted apartment building now called Crestview Condominiums. What could have been rented back in the seventies now had to be purchased outright or leased from an absentee owner on a who-knows-what kind of arrangement.

There was nothing particularly distinctive about the complex. It looked like a hundred other such structures dotting the West Hollywood hills. Nondescript tan concrete, enclosed balconies, underground garage, security gates, iron fence surrounding the perimeter. The place had the country club atmosphere of a minimum security federal penitentiary. Without the perks.

Large oak trees shielded the street from the cancerous rays of the Southern California sun. As I slid the Cadillac in next to the curb, I noticed a long-haired boy, wearing only a body shirt and cutoffs, rolling down the hill on a skateboard. By the time Lee and I vacated the car, the boy had made a gravity-defying swiveled leap over a garbage can and had disappeared down a paved alley between Conover's building and its next-door twin.

"I wonder if that's now the preferred mode of transportation for drug pushers, hustlers, and sneak thieves," I said.

"Aren't you being awfully cynical?" Lee said. "For all you know, that boy has perfectly valid reasons for being in that alley."

"Yeah, and they're all bad."

Lee laughed. "You've been reading too many paranoid thrillers." Then she grabbed my right elbow and guided me up the steps. "Besides, we've got other things to worry about."

"Like what?" I asked, as she pressed the buzzer to Conover's unit.

"Like blackmail, for one."

"Like what?" The tinny voice coming over the speaker momentarily startled us both.

"Mr. Conover?" Lee quickly covered her gaffe. "This is Lee Holland."

"Who?"

"Izzy sent me. Remember? We set up a four o'clock meeting."

"Oh yeah. Come on up. Take the elevator to the third floor. I'm the first door on the left."

We entered the foyer and immediately discovered that the building's interior was even less distinguished than its exterior. Somebody's idea of decor had been to situate a plastic potted plant in the corner and a Jackson Pollock print on the wall. The elevator door provided the only break to the depressing grayish lime color scheme. It was pink. Hot pink.

"Nice," I said, as the shocking door slid silently closed behind us.

Lee pinched me. "Will you please behave yourself?"

"Ow! How can I?" I said, rubbing my arm. "This is good old L.A."

She frowned but refrained from further comment. The elevator jolted to a stop, and the door opened to reveal a somewhat more cheerful landscape. The walls here were painted a more acceptable teal blue, and the carpet was mauve. I turned to check out the elevator door. This time it was burgundy. Go figure.

Conover's door opened almost immediately to Lee's knock. A man bearing a striking resemblance to the album pictures stood in the entryway. Even with the weathered lines in his face, Conover still possessed a youthful quality that magically recalled the eighteen-year-old boy of Izzy's photos.

"Hi," he said. Conover wore a periwinkle blue shirt over white chinos. Brown sandals completed his casual look. "Come on in."

Lee and I stepped over the threshold, closing the door behind us, and followed Conover into his apartment, accepting a guided tour as we went. It was brief.

"Here's the kitchen." A sink filled with unwashed dishes. Every inch of counter space covered with beer cans, empty microwavable packages, and discarded paper towels. Trash spilling out the receptacle, littering the floor. Kibble scattered in the corners.

"I'm not much of a housekeeper," he said.

"Understatement of the year, I'd call it," I muttered under my breath. Lee pinched me again.

"What's that?" he asked.

"Nothing," I answered, scowling at Lee. She pinches me again, I'm going to pinch her back, I silently vowed. "Nothing at all."

A fifty-five-gallon aquarium sat on the long bar that separated the kitchen from the living area.

"Please have a seat." Conover indicated a blue-gray sectional sofa, with a blue-gray seascape hanging above it. Blue-gray carpet and blue-gray walls completed the imaginative color scheme.

Lee and I perched on the edge of the sofa. Across the way I glimpsed a bed, a step up from the level of the living room, sheets awry, pillows on the floor. Conover followed my line of vision, said "Excuse me," walked over, and pulled together blue-gray draperies to hide the disorder from view. The decorator had at least been consistent, I thought.

"Like I said, I'm not much of a housekeeper." Conover shoveled newspapers off a La-Z-Boy and sat down across from the sofa. "You said on the phone you had a message or something for me from Izzy?"

While Lee explained the nature of our visit, my eyes moved around the room, seeing little I hadn't already noted. Except for the floor-to-ceiling plate-glass windows, which exposed an enclosed patio. A young man lay naked on the wood shingles above the Jacuzzi, soaking up the sun. A skateboard was turned upside down on the synthetic turf. My sneak thief, I thought.

I turned my attention back to Conover when he scoffed at the notion of blackmail.

"Do you have any idea what I do for a living?" he asked Lee after his laughing fit subsided.

"I assume you're still an actor," she answered.

"Oh, I am." Conover rose from his seat, walked over to the television cabinet, pulled out a videocassette, and brought it back to Lee. "This is just a sample." From the angle that Lee held the tape, I could read the title—*Bosun Buddies*—and the rating on the package cover—XXX.

I lifted the videotape from Lee's grasp. The jacket illustration didn't leave much to the imagination. Conover, dressed in a regulation white uniform with navy insignia, stood on the deck of a yacht, his fly open.

"Why don't you get star billing?" I asked, scanning down the men's names featured on the box—Cameron Cord, Greg Lennox, Lon Noll, Nick Edwards, Jason Foxx, Geof Hardin.

"Whaddya mean?"

"You're not even listed here in the credits."

"Oh, that." He smiled. "Read off the first name, the one right under the title."

"Cameron Cord," I said. "Is that you?"

"Sure." He nodded. "I took it from Camcord. Clever, huh?"

"Oh, yeah. Real clever." But I could tell my sarcasm was wasted on Conover.

"Nobody ever uses their real names in skinflicks," he explained, unfazed. "So, we either turn our real names inside out or just make up names to suit ourselves. Me, I guess I musta had half a dozen different names over the years."

"Doesn't that get confusing?" Lee asked.

"To whom?" he answered, as he reclaimed his seat.

"Never mind," I said.

"Look, I'll try to make it real easy for you to understand," Conover said. "I make porn. Period. And I like it. Being the final letter in Izzy's little alphabet wasn't even the first time. So, do you think some homemade crap from twenty years ago is gonna pull my chain? Get real."

"Aren't you a little old for this sort of thing?" I handed the tape back to Lee.

"Look, man, I do what I have to. What I know. What I do

best. Anyway," he stretched back in the cushioned recliner, "I'm gonna get into the production side. I have a big deal working even as we speak. Won't have to worry about keeping the weight off then." Conover slapped his stomach with both hands.

A knock against the glass interrupted his posturing. The young man stood at the plated window. Conover got up, walked over to the glass door, and slid it open.

"Gimme some stash," the young man demanded.

"Look, I've got company. And put on some clothes, for chrissakes."

"You gonna give me the stash, or what?"

"Five minutes, okay?"

"Five minutes, or I walk." The young man then turned, sauntered casually over to the Jacuzzi, and stepped gingerly into the water.

Conover turned back to us. "A friend of mine," he said. "Sorry."

"Look, we really have to be going," Lee said, fumbling with her purse. She pulled out a notebook and pencil, talking while she wrote. "We'll be at the Bonaventure for the next couple of days. Room eleven seventy-four. After that, you can reach us here." She tore off a sheet of paper and handed it to Conover. "I've listed both our addresses and phone numbers. Please let us know if anyone contacts you about that tape." Lee stood up.

"Sure thing. But I thought you said something about a gift?"

"Oh yes," Lee answered, and dug into her purse again. "Here."

Conover took the little box, held it up to his right ear, and shook it. "It's not a bomb, is it?" He laughed.

"It's from Izzy," Lee said.

"Then it probably is a bomb."

Lee snapped her purse shut. "Izzy just wanted you to have a remembrance from him," she said. "Plus, he wanted to let you know not to worry about those films anymore. He's going to destroy them before they land in somebody else's wrong hands."

"No skin off my nose," he said.

"Well, then, good-bye," Lee said, as we both stood up and headed toward the kitchen.

Conover didn't bother walking us out, didn't even look up. And he didn't show much more interest in Izzy's package. I saw him toss it casually toward the bed and watched in horror as it hit the floor instead.

"Tell Izzy hi for me." Conover finally remembered some manners as I opened the door for Lee and we walked into the hallway. The door closed behind us on his final words.

"Helluva great guy," he called.

* * *

"Can you imagine living that kind of life?" Lee asked as we waited for the elevator.

I shook my head. "That kid couldn't have been more than fifteen or sixteen," I said.

"And so brazen. I don't shock easily, but he just stood there. Didn't care at all what we thought."

"And we sure know what he meant by stash," I said.

Lee nodded. "Yeah. Drugs."

"Given Conover's past history, that wouldn't surprise me a bit," I said. "But why did you tell him Izzy was going to destroy the films? You know Izzy can't bring himself to do that."

"When I talked to Izzy yesterday," Lee said, "Izzy told me he'd decided to go ahead and get rid of the films, before they caused any more trouble."

"Conover didn't seem to care one way or the other," I said.

"Well, Kyle, you had Conover pegged, all right. He was a real jerk. I just don't understand why Izzy ever got mixed up with him in the first place."

"Well, Lee, you have to remember that Izzy handled him as a child star. He may not have been too bad back then."

"I wouldn't be so sure. Something tells me that he was probably a brat." Lee laughed.

"Well, I just hope the next guy is a little bit more normal. What's his name again?"

"Cash Hardesty."

I groaned. With a name like that, who knew what we'd be getting into.

CHAPTER 10

*"With biting and merciless satire,
the author
pokes good-natured fun
at our national preoccupation
with celebrity
and spares no one
in his cynical bashing."*

—Stokes Moran,
on Jim Stinson's *TV Safe*

Cash Hardesty's first words at least offered the promise of a more conventional interview.

"I'm sorry I was so abrupt with you on the phone," he said to Lee, "but I'm really in a rush today. You see, I have to catch a plane for New York in just under two hours. So I can't give you much time at all."

"No problem," Lee assured him.

"I'm afraid this was the only time I had left," he said as he ushered us inside his front door. Hardesty lived in a one-bedroom bungalow just north of Sunset. The house was small, but quite practical for a bachelor like Hardesty. "I hope seven o'clock wasn't too inconvenient."

Not inconvenient at all, as it had turned out. The Conover visit had been so much more abbreviated than we had anticipated that Lee and I found ourselves with time to spare. I suggested we drive into Beverly Hills for an early dinner at Chasen's. Lee proposed that we use the time to contact the four other men on Izzy's list and set tomorrow's schedule. We compromised by eating at Bob's Big Boy, where I ordered burgers while Lee made telephone calls.

"Success," Lee said, as she plopped down beside me on the restaurant's vinyl bench. "Three out of the four will see us tomorrow."

"What about the fourth?"

"Phone's been disconnected."

"Whose?"

"Robert Mallory. Long Beach."

This was even worse news than an outright refusal to meet with us, which we had anticipated from at least one of the men. A disconnected phone could mean any number of things, none of them encouraging. But what made my dark mood blacker was that it meant we'd have to risk a wasted trip to Long Beach with absolutely no guarantee of finding Mallory once we got there. Assuming, that is, that Lee insisted we make the effort. Which, of course, I knew she would.

I tuned back to my present surroundings just as Lee was finishing up with the preliminary explanations. "So you see," Lee was saying, "Izzy was concerned you might be subjected to some sort of extortion."

"I can't believe it," Hardesty said, slumping back against the wall. By mutual agreement, we stood in Hardesty's entryway, his two packed bags at his feet. Lee had promised we'd only take a minute. "I haven't thought about that film in over thirty years. And you say there were others involved as well."

"Yes," Lee answered, "but I'm sure you understand I'm not at liberty to reveal who. Or how many."

"Certainly," he answered, "I wouldn't expect you to. It just never occurred to me that what happened that night with Izzy and Lev was anything more than a spur of the moment kind of thing. I had no idea they were making a collection, or that I was a trophy to be hung on Izzy's wall."

"It wasn't quite that way," Lee said.

"Then how was it exactly?" Hardesty was becoming visibly angry. "Celebrity porno? I should imagine there's quite a market for that. I'm surprised Izzy hasn't cashed in on it himself. 'Sex Styles of the Rich and Famous.' He'd make a killing."

"Would something like this damage your career?" I asked cautiously, not wanting to further enrage the man.

"Well, it wouldn't help, that's for sure."

Hardesty currently starred in "Forever Love," an afternoon soap where he played the part of the family patriarch. That role had provided his primary livelihood for the past fourteen years. But in the early sixties, Hardesty had starred in half a dozen big-budget romantic melodramas, cast more due to his rugged good looks than for any particular acting talent. At the time, those films had made Hardesty one of the hottest properties in Hollywood and the idol of millions of teenage girls. Lee had culled all this information from Izzy's notes and shared it with me on the drive over.

I assessed Hardesty's current physical appearance, as opposed to the young stallion of Izzy's album. His leonine white hair made him look older than his fifty-three years, and forty or so pounds had been added to the athletic build that at one time had sent adoring fans into ecstasy. Still, he retained an undeniable magnetism. Even when not at his most charming. Like now.

"So no one has contacted you about the tape?" Lee asked.

"Just you. Isn't this ironic? Tomorrow three heartthrobs from the sixties—me, Tory Andrews, and Fairlane Jeffries—will be filming a commercial for Tasty Cola's Ultimate Experience Pizza Parlors, a where-are-they-now kind of thing. You can imagine how fast the sponsors would drop me if something like this came out."

"Why?" I asked. "It was more than thirty years ago. Would it really make that much of a difference today?"

"You tell me," Hardesty said contemptuously. "There's not much call for a queer ladies' man, now is there?"

"I take it, then, that you're not gay, Mr. Hardesty?" Lee asked.

"Not on your life, sister. What went down that night with Izzy and Lev happened strictly because I was drunk. If I had been sober, I never would have done it. Not in a million years." His face flushed, Hardesty added, "But snockered as I was, it just seemed like a little harmless horseplay. Or, at least, that's all I thought it was."

"How long will you be in New York?" Lee asked, abruptly changing the conversational direction. Too abruptly, I thought. Lee, don't be so obvious, I inwardly warned.

"They've blocked off two days—" Hardesty began, then asked suspiciously, "Why do you want to know?"

I knew what wheels were turning in Lee's head. If we could get back to New York in time, Lee and I could interview Andrews and Jeffries, the only two non-Californians on our list. But Lee couldn't volunteer that information to Hardesty. I wondered how long it would take him to figure it out.

"We're only staying at the Bonaventure for a couple of more days," Lee said. "If by any chance you are contacted about that tape, you can reach us at our home addresses. Let me write them down for you." She opened her handbag, seemed suddenly flustered, and turned back to Hardesty. "Do you have pen and paper? I seem to be out."

While Hardesty went to retrieve the items from the other room, I gave Lee a quizzical look. She tipped her purse at an angle and held it open in my direction. *Bosun Buddies* leered obscenely back at me.

"How—" I started to ask, but I immediately cut my question off at Hardesty's return.

Lee shook her head as he handed her the pen and paper. "You'll have to forgive me," she said, as she wrote out the information for him, "I'm usually better prepared. Here." She tore off the page and placed it in his hand. "Please get in touch with us if you hear anything. All right?"

"Okay," he promised. "But if somebody thinks they can blackmail me, they'd better have a lot of health insurance and maybe even a good life insurance policy."

"I'm sorry this has been so upsetting to you," Lee said, "and Izzy wants you to know that the film will be destroyed. I can promise you he doesn't want something like this happening again."

"I should hope not," Hardesty said. "I wish I'd never heard about it. Right now, I even wish I'd never heard of Izzy Cohen."

"Well, thanks for meeting with us anyway," Lee said as she opened the door. "Oh, by the way, I have a gift for you from Izzy." She held her bag close to her chest, rummaged carefully through its contents, and brought out the small package. She extended it to Hardesty.

"Keep it," he said. "I don't want anything from Izzy. Not any more."

"I'm sorry you feel that way, but there's no way I can keep it. I promised Izzy I'd give it to you. I'll just put it here on this table, and you can do with it whatever you like."

"I'll just toss it in the garbage," he said.

"Fine," Lee responded. "It's certainly yours to do with as you please."

I stepped out on the bungalow's porch. Lee turned on the stoop and said smilingly, "Have a nice trip, Mr. Hardesty."

"Not much hope of that now." Then the door banged shut behind us.

* * *

"How did that tape get in your bag?" I demanded when we were safely back in the car.

"How should I know?" Lee said.

"Well, it didn't get in there all by itself."

"All I can think is that I must have accidentally slipped it in there in my rush to get out of Conover's apartment."

"Oh, sure."

"Are you saying that I took it deliberately?"

"Well, it's a little big not to notice," I said. "And how come you didn't realize it was there when you made those calls at the restaurant?"

Lee's eyes flashed fire. "I keep my change in my wallet. Which I carry in my jacket pocket." To prove her point, she pulled the item from her jacket and waved it in my face. "And, from the time we left Conover's, I didn't open my bag again until we were there in Hardesty's apartment."

"Oh, so now you're saying Conover sneaked it into your purse when you weren't looking."

"No, I'm not saying that. More than likely, I did stick it in there." Then, with a somewhat softer tone, her anger evaporated, she added, "But I didn't mean to."

"Great," I said, as I steered the Cadillac down Sunset. "What do we do with it now?"

"Maybe we'll have an opportunity to return it to Conover," Lee said.

"Yeah, like I'm sure either one of us wants to meet up with him again."

Lee and I lapsed into silence for several blocks. As I directed the Cadillac onto the freeway entry ramp, Lee commented, "You know, two men couldn't be more different than Conover and Hardesty. One is too eager to embrace his sexual nature while the other is just as quick to reject it."

"You think Hardesty's still in the closet?"

"I think it's possible. Anyone who's that spirited in his denial is bound to be hiding something."

"Yeah," I agreed. "But what?"

"And the even more important question for us—" Lee continued, then broke off.

"Yes?" I said.

"If Hardesty is hiding something, does it have anything to do with the missing tape?"

I nodded. "And there's something else that doesn't quite add up, either," I said. "Hardesty has a steady income from that soap of his. You'd think he'd be able to afford a better place to live. That bungalow—"

"Was a dump," Lee supplied succinctly.

"I wouldn't go that far," I argued, shifting the Cadillac over into the downtown exit lane. "But I will say that it obviously seemed beneath what you'd assume his financial means would allow. So that makes me wonder, why does Hardesty live like that?"

"Not to mention," Lee said, "what he actually does with all his money?"

"Exactly."

But those questions seemingly had no answers. At least not for the moment. Not for tonight.

Tomorrow, Lee and I would have three more opportunities to get to the bottom of this mystery. Three more of Izzy's former clients. If Conover and Hardesty had been any indication, tomorrow's interviews promised to be real corkers.

I couldn't wait.

C H A P T E R 1 1

"The novel is filled
with marvelous characters,
packed
with delightful repartee,
and charged with comic energy."

—Stokes Moran,
on Samuel Holt's
The Fourth Dimension Is Death

It was after eight P.M. when we got back to the Bonaventure. Lee checked at the front desk for messages, but there were none. Since we had eaten at Bob's Big Boy around five o'clock, we elected to bypass the restaurant, hoping that we would not be starving to death in a couple hours' time. With nothing else on the night's agenda, we went to our room.

A fax awaited Lee's return. She tore it off the machine and announced excitedly, "They bought it. And they're offering a fifty thousand dollar advance."

I grabbed her by the waist and whirled her around. "That's wonderful," I said. "This has to be some kind of record. You sent the proposal off at what time?"

"About two-thirty, I think," Lee said, when she had regained her footing.

"And what time did the answer come back?"

"Let's see." Lee examined the paper for a report of its transmission. "It says five forty-five. But I don't know if that's our time, or their time."

"Well, they either snapped it up in fifteen minutes, or three hours and fifteen minutes. Either way, it's a miracle."

"It is that," Lee agreed. "I've heard of fast deals before, but nothing like this."

"Well, fax them back our acceptance."

Lee wavered. "It's after eleven o'clock their time. No one will be there."

"Doesn't matter," I said. "Then they'll just find it waiting for them first thing in the morning. Go ahead. Send it."

"All right," Lee agreed, as she wrote out the response. "But you know what this means, don't you? You'll have to get to work on the book right away."

I smiled. "Don't worry. I've already added two more titles to my ten favorites list."

"Oh, that is progress."

"Now don't be snide. I want you to know that I'm taking this assignment very seriously."

Lee placed the paper in the machine, programmed the number, and hit the Transmit key. I could hear the automatic dialing as she walked over to where I sat on the edge of the bed.

"I'm glad you're taking it seriously," she said. "So am I." She planted a kiss on my cheek.

"This still doesn't seem real," I said. "I can't believe I'll be able to hold in my hands a book with my name on it. And by Christmas, no less."

"You won't have anything unless you get a move on," she said. "So what are the two latest additions you've made to your list?"

"Well, I couldn't very well have a favorites list without including Sherlock Holmes. Especially considering the fact that I borrowed the name Stokes Moran from *The Adventure of the Speckled Band*. So," I waited for an imaginary drumroll, "I'm including *The Hound of the Baskervilles*."

"That's pretty predictable, isn't it?" Lee said.

"Predictable or not, it does happen to be one of my favorites. Not to mention that it's also one of the great mysteries of all time."

"But wouldn't Wilkie Collins' *The Moonstone* be just as representative?" Lee said, now sitting cross-legged on the bed. "And nowhere near as predictable."

"Fine," I answered. "You put Collins on your list. But I'm keeping Conan Doyle on mine."

"This is wonderful," she said, clapping her hands together. "This type of debate is exactly what your list should generate. You'll have some readers agreeing with you, some upset with your choices, and others ready to kill you." Lee smiled. "It'll be great."

"I'm not so sure," I acknowledged. "Whether you were aware of it or not, I was getting a little bit angry just now."

"Angry? I'd say furious was more like it." She crawled over to where I was sitting and nuzzled my neck. "Admit it."

"How can I admit anything when you're doing that?" I pulled her into my arms and cradled her head against my chest.

"What's your other choice?"

"This." I bent down and kissed her.

"No, silly," she said when our lips parted. "I meant for your list."

"Oh, that. *The List of Adrian Messenger* by Philip MacDonald. Seems appropriate since we're right now tracking down a list of names for Izzy."

"But those on our list are still very much alive."

"For the time being," I said.

"What's that supposed to mean?" Lee giggled, more I imagined from the route of my hands than from the humor of my words.

"How should I know?" I kissed her again. "It was just something to say," I whispered behind her ear.

Lee pushed herself away from my embrace. "But that's still only four titles. You're going too slow."

"I thought you liked it when I went slow." I reached out for her, but she eluded my grasp.

"Not this time. Add another book to your list. Right now. With no hesitation. What comes immediately to mind?"

"You." I lunged again. This time I caught her.

"Seriously," she repeated when we broke for air. "Another book that you know should be on your list."

"*The Affair of the Blood-Stained Egg Cosy*."

Lee frowned. "I never heard of it."

"It's a wonderful English mystery by James Anderson, a delightful pastiche of the classic nineteen thirties country house murders. It's got everything—list of suspects, floor plans, secret passages."

"It sounds divine. How come you've never recommended it to me?"

"The book came out before I started reviewing. I guess I just never thought to mention it to you."

"But you're sure it's one of your favorites?"

"Absolutely."

"Good," she applauded. "Now you only have five more to go. That wasn't that hard, was it?"

I swept Lee up in my arms. "Not at all," I admitted. "But something else certainly is." We fell back onto the bed, laughing together.

The rest of the list, as well as everything else, would just have to wait.

C H A P T E R   1 2

"The author
nails Los Angeles,
a bull's-eye indictment
of get-rich-quick schemes
and the quest
for the good life."

—Stokes Moran,
on Faye Kellerman's *Milk and Honey*

"*I* thought it never rained in Southern California," Lee said glumly.

"That's what the chamber of commerce would have you believe."

"Then what happened?"

"They lie," I said.

Contrary to popular thinking, winter rains are not a rarity in Los Angeles. In fact, the entire basin gets a fair amount of precipitation between the months of October and March. Not every day, mind you, but enough to occasionally wipe away the smog and keep the fire trucks at bay. Except during periods of prolonged drought. Like the nineteen eighties.

I always liked seeing the rains come when I lived out here.

But not what the rain did to the traffic, of course. Californians don't have the least notion how to drive when water meets asphalt. This morning my mood matched Lee's only because the clouds picked the one day we'd be driving all over creation to spill their guts. Which made surviving these streets all the more difficult.

Concentrating on the road in this downpour was giving me a headache, not to mention that during my first fifteen minutes behind the wheel three idiot drivers had already made death-defying U-turns right in front of me. I was ready to strangle Max Morgan the minute we found him. Not content to meet us at his real estate office in Sherman Oaks, he had instead asked that we rendezvous at a property he was showing in Tarzana. I briefly shifted my eyes away from the liquid windshield and momentarily glared at Lee. She was the one who had agreed to Morgan's mad request in the first place.

I turned left off Ventura Boulevard, determined to concentrate on locating the address he had given. It wasn't easy. Reading the street signs proved virtually impossible in this deluge. But with Lee's help, I finally got the Cadillac on the correct street, and shortly thereafter I pulled to a stop in front of what I hoped was the right house. We were thirty-five minutes late.

"I hope he's still here," Lee said, glancing at her watch.

"If he's not, he will die," I promised.

"What?" Lee asked.

"Nothing," I said. "Maybe we should wait a couple of minutes for the rain to ease up."

"Kyle, we've been driving in this mess for more than an hour with no let-up in sight. At the rate it's coming down, I doubt there'll be any drastic change in the next ten years."

"We're going to get soaked," I said. Neither one of us had possessed sufficient imagination to think to bring umbrellas with us from New York.

"Then we'll get soaked. Look, we're already late. You can stay here if you want, but I'm going in." With that, she opened the door and bolted out into the rain.

"Aw, shit," I said, and bolted after her.

* * *

Luckily for him, Max Morgan was there. I wouldn't have to murder him after all, maybe just hurt him a little. I pondered an appropriate revenge as Lee and I stood in the empty living room watering the carpet. Morgan had gone to find towels.

"I'm afraid this is all there was," he said, walking back into the room. Morgan held a roll of bathroom tissue in one hand and a box of Kleenex in the other. I grabbed the roll and gave Lee the box.

"I'm sorry there's no place to sit down." Morgan talked while Lee and I dabbed the water off our faces.

"If I'd known it was gonna come a gully washer today, I wouldn't have suggested you come all the way out here," he apologized. Lee and I were not having much success with the flimsy paper. Trying to dry our soaking clothes and hair was a lost cause.

"But I had already scheduled a nine o'clock appointment

with a prospective client, as well as an eleven o'clock," Morgan continued. "The nine o'clock didn't show, and I doubt the eleven will either. Can't blame 'em. So it definitely looks like all three of us wasted a trip."

"All we wanted was to speak to you privately," Lee said, looking around at the vacant house, "and we certainly accomplished that."

Morgan laughed. "Well, I'm glad you came, then. You wanna look around the place while we talk?" he said. "I know you're not buyers, but it probably beats standing in one spot."

"That sounds fine," Lee answered. "How is business anyway? I mean, when it's not raining."

"Pretty lousy, if you want the truth. The last three years have been a nightmare. The eighties boomed, and then when the nineties hit, the bottom just fell out."

Morgan led us through the kitchen while Lee explained the nature of our visit.

"Oh, little lady, I am so ashamed of that, I can't begin to tell you," Morgan stated. "If my wife ever found out, she'd divorce me in no time flat. And we've been married almost forty years."

According to Izzy's notes, Morgan had been a down-on-his-luck stand-up comic when Izzy discovered him in a seedy nightclub in Hollywood. Something clicked for Izzy, though, and he saw in Morgan the makings of a major talent. Izzy landed him comedy parts in a few movies, but Morgan's real break, and lasting fame, came with his own television variety series in the mid-fifties. But when the show finally left the air after a successful seven-year run, Morgan gradually disappeared from public view.

Looking at the man today, it was impossible to see any resemblance to the pictures in Izzy's album. Morgan was now in his early sixties, almost bald except for some tufts of white hair on the sides and back of his head, and he gave a pretty fair imitation of Tommy Lasorda before Ultra Slimfast. In addition, his full lips seemed a perfect repository for a fat two-dollar cigar.

But, unlike the two men in our interviews the previous day, Max Morgan was as nice and down-home as his Indiana roots.

"So you haven't been contacted by anyone trying to extort money from you over that film?" Lee asked, as we walked through the side hallway toward the stairs.

"No ma'am," Morgan said. "And if I am, I don't know what I'll do. I guess I'll either give them every cent I've got. Or maybe I'll kill them, or myself, or both."

Morgan reached in his back pants pocket, brought out his wallet, and opened it for us to see. "My three kids are all grown now," he said, "but I still carry their pictures with me wherever I go." He flipped through photos of two men and a woman. Then he showed us pictures of two small children. "And here's my grandson and granddaughter."

Morgan stuffed his wallet back in his trousers. "I can't let anything hurt my family," he said, his voice cracking. Morgan pulled a wrinkled handkerchief from inside his sports coat and brushed at the corners of his eyes. "And you better believe my boss would drop me flat. I know this job's not much, but it's all I have. I'm too old to start all over again," he sobbed. "If this comes out, I'll lose everything."

I watched this pathetic scene with mixed reactions. Touching as his plight was, I couldn't forget that Morgan had been an accomplished showman at one time in his life. Was he genuinely expressing his emotions, or was he just giving a hokey performance to a gullible audience? And if it were the latter, did it really make any difference?

"Do you mind my asking why you made the film in the first place?" Lee asked. The three of us now stood on the up-stairs landing.

"You've heard the old joke about starving comics," Morgan said. "Well, for me it was no joke. When Izzy found me, I didn't have two cents to rub together. I'd have gone back home to South Bend, but I didn't have the price of the ticket. Izzy took me in, and he and Lev treated me like I was some-body special. I hadn't felt that way in so long I guess I'da done just about anything they wanted." He paused, then grinned and sheepishly added, "And I guess I did."

"So it wasn't to further your career?" I asked.

"Good lord, no," he replied. "What career? At that time, I was strictly a nobody. Success came later—Izzy representing me, getting me jobs, selling me to the TV producers, all that came afterward. No, Izzy didn't have to do all that if what he wanted was . . . " and here he struggled with the word . . . "sex. He had already gotten that."

I frowned. This account did not fit with my preconceived

opinions. Maybe Lee had been right, and there had been no coercion. Somehow, though, I couldn't quite let go of my prior conviction.

We walked silently through the bedrooms, phony buyers in a fake dream. Finally, we headed back down the stairs.

"Thank you so much for talking with us, Mr. Morgan," Lee said, standing at the front door. "But please get in touch with us if you do hear anything?" She handed him a slip of paper. This morning, after she had called Izzy to report on yesterday's activities and before we left the hotel room, Lee had written out our names, addresses, and phone numbers on four sheets of paper, rather than fumble with this moment like yesterday.

"Oh, I almost forgot," Lee added, "Izzy asked me to give you something." She reached into her purse, brought out the small package, and extended it toward Morgan. This was the third time she had "almost forgot." Her technique was getting stale, and I wondered why she was constantly repeating it.

"No ma'am," he said with finality, "I don't want it. I haven't needed anything from Izzy Cohen in over thirty years, and I'm not about to take something now. You keep it."

"But I can't," Lee protested. "Please take it."

But Morgan was adamant. "Then throw it away," he said.

"But you don't even know what it is," Lee pleaded.

"Whatever it is," Morgan said, "I can live without it. I have so far."

* * *

"Open it," I demanded, as soon as we were back in the car. The rain had not let up in the least, and we had found ourselves once again in mother nature's rinse cycle.

"No," Lee refused, "I don't feel right about opening it. Izzy didn't intend for us to know what's in here." She still held the package in her hand.

"He didn't intend for it to be thrown away, either," I said.

"I'm not going to throw it away."

"Then what are you going to do with it?"

"I'm going to return it to Izzy."

I thought about that for a minute. "Are you sure that's wise?" I finally asked. "The fact that Morgan refused to accept it might really upset Izzy."

Lee considered my argument, then nodded. "You're right," she admitted. "It just might."

"And you wouldn't want to take that chance, would you?" I pressed my advantage.

"No, I wouldn't."

"Then go ahead. Open it."

"All right, you've convinced me." Lee laughed. "Plus, I'm as curious to see what's in here as you are."

"Just one thing," I said, while Lee was struggling to unfasten the taped edges. "Why did you accept the package back from Morgan, but not from Hardesty yesterday?"

"Maybe because I believed Morgan when he said he wouldn't accept it." She finally just tore apart the paper, opened the box, and retrieved a piece of purple stationery. She unfolded it. A key was taped to the top.

"What's it say?" I asked excitedly.

"Dear Max," Lee read, "I'm truly sorry for all the trouble I've caused. Maybe this key will make some amends. I told Lee I was going to destroy the film, but after thinking that over, I realized I didn't have the right. It's not just because of Lev; that film is a record of your life as well. It's up to you to decide what's to be done with it.

"This key opens a safety deposit box at Chase Manhattan Bank on East Sixty-second Street in New York City. The number of the box is imprinted on the key. Inside that box is your film. Do with it as you will."

Lee gently lowered the paper. "And it's signed, Izzy," she finished.

"Well, now we know," I said, experiencing a sudden melancholy.

Lee nodded her head. "Yes," she sighed, "now we know."

CHAPTER 13

*"This Hollywood novel
has everything—
memorable characters,
irresistible plotting,
and plenty of show business gossip."*

— Stokes Moran,
on Stan Cutler's
Best Performance by a Patsy

"Don't you think it's time we cut our losses?"

"What do you mean?"

"It seems fairly obvious to me that Ted Nichols is not trying to use that tape to blackmail anyone," I said.

"We still have five men to see," Lee protested, "three here in L.A. and two more, if we can get there in time, when we get back to New York. Any one of them might have been contacted. I think it's too early to call it quits. Who knows? We may just have started from the wrong end, that's all."

"I don't agree," I argued. "I think this whole trip has been not only a waste of our time but of Izzy's money as well. And what do we have to show for our efforts? Nothing, absolutely zilch. So far, it's been a total washout." Then, as the

Cadillac hit yet another pothole, I added somewhat sarcastically, "And I don't just mean this god-awful road."

This morning, before we had left our hotel, Lee and I had agreed that the only good thing about driving all the way out to Tarzana to meet with Morgan was that afterward we could cut across to Malibu on Topanga Canyon Boulevard. But that, of course, was before the rains came.

Visibility was bad enough in the heavy downpour, which, if anything, had increased in intensity since we had left the relative safety of Ventura Boulevard. But trying to maneuver this ark of an automobile through the treacherous hairpin turns of this winding mountain road, with its narrow shoulders and sudden bumps, was a foolhardy challenge even Evel Knievel would have foregone. The Cadillac hugged the center line. To our left, the cliff face stood in rugged profile, the rock raw and exposed, where man and machines had hacked out this fragile path. Luckily, the terror on the right wasn't visible at all, the sightline where the terrain abruptly fell away lost instead in a bottomless sea of gray mist. But we knew what was there, some five hundred feet below us. Just waiting for the careless, the unwary.

"Will you please slow down?" Lee shrieked, as the big car skidded on another turn, sloughing on the soggy soil.

"I'm only going thirty-five," I answered.

"Well, it's still too fast." Lee gripped her armrest with the rictus of death. "Cut your speed. Now!"

I eased off the accelerator, watched the digital readout drop to thirty. "We'll never get there at this rate," I said.

"We'll never get there at any rate, if you're not more careful."

"All right," I said, "I'll put it on twenty-five."

"Thank you." Lee's voice was heavy with sarcasm, but I saw the tension on her armrest ease. I grinned. Safe and steady, said the tortoise.

"Since this trip's now going to take us forever, why don't you tell me about the next loser on our list?"

"Toby Vickers is not a loser," Lee said. "He was one of Izzy's most successful clients. Back in the mid-sixties, he starred in a series of very popular beach movies. Then he made the transition to television in a prime-time medical drama. Now he emcees a daytime game show. He's hardly been out of work a day in the last three decades."

"Oh, I'm impressed," I said.

"Well, you should be. According to Izzy's notes, Toby is genuinely a nice guy. Not like some others I could mention."

Then Lee added, somewhat archly, "Present company not excluded."

"What's that supposed to mean?"

"Well, since you asked, I think you've gone out of your way to make this trip miserable. Finding fault with everything and everyone. I'd occasionally like to hear a kind word among all the harsh ones."

Lee was right, of course. This time out, L.A. and I had not hit it off, and I had made absolutely no effort to correct it. After fifteen years, I couldn't order the city to suddenly shift backward, just to fit my fixed memory, and I had been taking out my frustration on Lee. She deserved better treatment from me, and she had every right to expect it. I had been behaving like a petulant child.

"I'm sorry," I said, and I meant it.

"That's okay." I could detect a softer tone in Lee's voice; perhaps even a smile lurked at the corners of her lips. "You've just been making it that much tougher on me."

"Well, if we ever get out of these mountains alive," I said, "remind me to make it up to you."

Lee laughed. "Don't worry, I will," she promised. Then she added, "Tonight."

* * *

Lee's earlier phone call to Toby Vickers had assured us access to the exclusive seaside community of Malibu. The guard at the south end of the hamlet's single street directed us to Vickers' place. As we drove down the wide boulevard, I could almost smell money in the air.

Some of the world's wealthiest, most famous, and most influential people routinely occupied this slim strip of sand fronting the Pacific Ocean. Behind those anonymous stucco facades lived movie stars, industry magnates, exiled potentates. Those modest doors opened onto lavish beach houses hoarding treasures beyond imagination. Beyond reach. By special invitation only.

Here, privacy was paramount. In other lives, these people might be public figures, but here no audience was ever granted to the masses. Here, neighbors didn't borrow cups of sugar, or hold block parties, or have garage sales. Here was exclusivity, blatant discrimination, overt hostility, acceptable separation from the rest of humanity. The quiet serene city screamed KEEP OUT!

The rented Cadillac suffered no inferiority complex cruising past the Ferraris, Lamborghinis, and Porsches. Nor did it hesitate in finally pulling to a stop in front of Toby Vickers' address. As I cut the engine, I secretly wished we had leased a Rent-a-Wreck instead. That would certainly have gotten the neighbors talking.

"What kind of crazy will we get this time?" I asked Lee as she joined me at Vickers' door. She answered with a noncommittal shrug.

Lee buzzed our presence, then we stood awaiting entry. Patiently waited. Lee buzzed again. And again. Several minutes elapsed. Fortunately, the rain had dropped to a mere drizzle, so by the time Vickers finally buzzed the door open, Lee and I were a little soggy but nowhere near as wet as we had been after our drenching at Morgan's place. But we were a lot angrier. Or at least one of us was, that is. Me.

"How dare he keep us cooling our heels like that?" I grumbled as we made our way down a covered walkway past a recessed rock garden. "And in the pouring rain."

"Kyle, be good. Maybe he had a good reason for not answering the bell immediately. Now, quiet, there he is." Lee nodded toward the entrance to the main house.

Vickers stood in the open doorway, toweling his wet hair. "I'm sorry if I kept you waiting," he apologized. "I was having a run on the beach with my dogs. I hope you weren't standing out there too long."

"No, no, not at all," Lee said.

Vickers moved back against the door frame. "Won't you come in?"

I followed Lee into the wide living area, while Vickers closed the door behind us. I hurriedly whispered, "Well, he did have a reason, though I don't know how good it was." Lee frowned and looked about ready to pinch me, so I moved out of harm's way.

"Won't you have a seat?" Vickers offered, gesturing toward the sectional sofa.

The living area was tastefully decorated in muted shades of teal and white. Three sides of the room were given over to floor-to-ceiling glass windows, showcasing a dramatic ocean vista. The fourth wall contained a brick-encased fireplace, with well-stocked bookshelves lining both sides. A copy of John Grisham's latest legal thriller lay faceup on the ebony cocktail table.

"Could I get you something to drink?" Vickers inquired, once Lee and I were comfortably nested.

"No, thank you," Lee answered. His question reminded me that we had yet to eat lunch, prompting a reflex sound from my stomach. I hoped no one heard.

"How is Izzy?"

"He's fine," Lee said. "He just celebrated his eightieth birthday."

While Lee and Vickers exchanged small talk, I took a

mental inventory of the man. Dressed in his black sweatsuit, his dark hair ruffled by the towel, Toby Vickers vibrated masculinity. Tall and good-looking, he possessed a casual air of self-confidence, more comforting than arrogant. His easy smile animated the crisp blue eyes. I agreed with Izzy. Toby Vickers seemed like a genuinely nice guy.

"I've got to tell you," Vickers said, when Lee had finished explaining the nature of our visit, "if this went public, it would definitely hurt. No doubt about it." He walked over to the wet bar and poured himself a hefty drink from a crystal decanter.

"I've lived with the possibility of blackmail almost all my adult life," Vickers said, as he perched on the end of the sofa opposite where Lee and I sat. "In this business, when you're homosexual, you just kind of always expect it." He stood up and walked over to the window.

"Down there on that beach somewhere are the three most important things in my life," he continued. "My lover, Scott, and my two shelties, Thelma and Louise. I know that no matter what else happens, I won't lose them."

Vickers turned back toward us. "I don't blame Izzy. I knew what I was doing. Let's see—I'm forty-nine now, and that was almost thirty years ago. I guess I was twenty or twenty-one at the time. So I was clearly of age."

"Why did you do it?" Lee asked softly.

"Everything was all so new to me then," he answered. "Hollywood, the movies, the whole business. Especially sex." He grinned. "I couldn't get enough, couldn't absorb it fast enough. I suppose the idea of filming sex was just another turn-on. I certainly don't remember objecting, or really ever having any second thoughts."

Vickers downed the liquid in his glass. "Until now, that is."

"What will you do if you're contacted?" I asked.

"I don't know. I don't like the whole idea of blackmail, and I would hate paying off such a scuzzball. But money's not important.

"We're well fixed here. Scott's a successful architect, and I've made wise investments over the years. Plus, I earn big bucks for the game show."

He sat once again at the end of the sofa. "I couldn't have a better deal. I only have to work one day a week. I go in to the studio one week a month and tape four weeks' worth of shows. And for that I earn more than a million dollars a year. Talk about an easy life."

Vickers lapsed into silence. After a moment, he said, a touch of sadness in his voice, "No, money's not the issue. I just have to decide if protecting my reputation is worth the cost of selling my soul."

Lee nudged me. I met her eyes and nodded. We rose in unison.

"Thank you for talking with us, Mr. Vickers," Lee said.

"Toby, please," he insisted, rising to his feet.

"Thank you, Toby. It's been a pleasure meeting you. I just wish it could have been under different circumstances."

Vickers extended his hand, first to Lee, then to me. "I should be the one thanking you," he said. "It's certainly a lot gentler hearing this from you than from some strange voice on the telephone. At least now I'm prepared."

Lee reached inside her handbag. "Izzy asked me to give you this," Lee said, as she withdrew the package.

"What is it?" Vickers asked, as he accepted the gift.

"It's something . . . " Lee stalled as she searched for the appropriate words. "From Izzy to you," she ended firmly.

"Please thank him for me," Vickers said as he opened the door for our exit. "And tell him everything's fine."

Lee nodded.

"You understand what I mean, don't you?" he asked.

Lee answered with a smile. "Yes," she said, as she leaned over and brushed a kiss against his right cheek. "Everything's fine."

* * *

"First things first," I said, as soon as we were both back in the car. "Let's eat."

"Sounds great to me," Lee said. "I'm starved."

"You have anything special in mind?" I asked, as I put the car in gear.

"How about some place in Long Beach?"

"Long Beach?" I exploded. "Right. You want to go all the way to Long Beach just for lunch."

She nodded.

"Bypass all the restaurants in Santa Monica," I continued, "Los Angeles, Inglewood, Compton, and points in between. Just so you can say you ate in Long Beach."

Lee nodded again. This time a grin spread across her lips.

"And, oh," I added, as I merged the Cadillac with other traffic on Pacific Coast Highway, "while we're there, we might as well stop off and see if we can track down Robert Mallory."

"Why Kyle, that's a wonderful idea." Lee laughed, clapping her hands together. "You're so considerate to make such a kind offer."

"Think nothing of it," I said, matching her laughter. "I'm just that kind of guy."

CHAPTER 14

"The author
allows the appealing characters
and the
lighthearted style
to gently
nudge the reader toward
the politically correct position."

—Stokes Moran,
on Susan Conant's *Gone to the Dogs*

*H*unger didn't make it to Long Beach.

Just outside Malibu, Lee spotted an inviting seaside restaurant and insisted that we stop. She didn't get any opposition from me.

The food was wonderful. A spinach salad, followed by lobster bisque, scampi, baked potatoes, and home-baked rolls, topped off with chocolate mousse and cappuccino. We devoured the meal in the glorious afternoon sun that had finally beaten away the rain, the warm rays streaming through the windows while the ocean lapped gently against the pilings under our feet. It was as close to heaven as I'd been this side of satin sheets.

Lee and I left the restaurant in a different frame of mind. Stomachs full and minds content, we were suffused with a fresh energy, a rekindled optimism. The long drive to Long Beach passed quickly, animated by a renewed zest both in our assignment and in each other. If we had been nearer our hotel, I'm certain what direction our mutual fire would have taken us. But, as it was, conversation had to suffice.

"Tell me about Robert Mallory," I suggested to Lee, as I turned the Cadillac off Pacific Coast Highway and on to Santa Monica Boulevard.

"He seems to be the least successful of all Izzy's clients," she answered, pulling Izzy's notes out of her handbag and thumbing through the pages until she located the section she sought. "Yes, it's just as I thought. Robert Mallory, or Bob as Izzy refers to him, only had one brief period of fame. He starred in a short-lived television series in the mid-sixties." She glanced over at me. "That seems to be about it."

"You mean that's all Izzy says?" I asked incredulously.

"No," Lee answered, "he mentions that Bob had a few problems but that generally he was pretty easy to work with."

"Problems? What problems?"

"Emotional, I guess. Izzy's not too clear about it."

"Well, just read me what he's written."

"Okay," she said, and then read, "Bob was very uptight, very high-strung, comfortable in front of the camera but a shambles the rest of the time. I never knew if it was a family thing, or drugs, or what. When his series folded, Bob became so unreliable I dropped him as a client. The last thing I told him was to see a psychiatrist." Lee's voice trailed into silence.

"Is that it?" I asked, changing lanes for the San Diego Freeway.

"Yes, that's everything I've got here."

"Then the address Izzy gave us for Mallory is twenty-five years old," I said with disbelief. "Talk about wild goose chases, this really is one."

"No, no, no," Lee corrected. "Because of residuals from the TV series, Izzy had to keep track of Mallory. The address was still good as of last summer."

"How do you know that?" I asked.

"It's right here in the back of the photo album." She lifted the book from the seat and extended it to me. "There's a dated notation in the margin next to Mallory's address."

"I can't look at that now," I said, keeping my eye on a big eighteen-wheeler that seemed to be having trouble staying in its lane. "It says all that about residuals?" I remained skeptical.

"No." Lee shook her head. "Izzy told me about residuals when we discussed all this a few days ago. And he also told me that the dates next to the men's names indicated the last time he had corresponded with them. Usually to forward residual payments." Lee seemed exasperated. "But that's not important. What I'm trying to get you to understand is that the address on Mallory was still good as recently as a few months ago."

"Well, why didn't you just say so?" I quipped. It's a good thing I had the steering wheel in my hands. If I hadn't been driving, Lee would have brained me.

* * *

"Here's Newport," I said, turning right at the four-way stop sign. "What number did you say?"

"Three twenty-one." Lee scoured house numbers on her side of the street. "There it is."

"Where?"

"That three-story apartment building right there. Slow down, stop, you're passing it," she screamed.

I eased the big car next to the curb.

"No harm done," I said, "it's just behind us."

Lee had her door open before I killed the motor, and she was already at the apartment house entrance by the time I stepped up on the sidewalk. I finally caught up with her in the building's lobby.

"There's no Mallory listed on the mailboxes," she said morosely.

"Well, what did you expect? His phone's been disconnected. I'd say that's a pretty good indicator he no longer lives here."

"What do we do now?"

Opposite from the elevator a doorsign announced Manager's Office. "Let's ask the manager," I suggested.

"Oh, you're so brilliant," she said, and poked me in the ribs.

"It was only obvious," I demurred. "Nothing Hercule Poirot wouldn't have thought of."

Lee laughed. "Just shut up, and knock on the damn door."

"Yes ma'am." We were both still laughing when the door opened and revealed a woman of herculean size. If the Green Bay Packers had ever fielded a female linebacker, this would have been the one. At least seventy years of age, and standing more than six feet tall, she weighed in excess of what had to be three hundred pounds. The only thing little-old-ladyish about the figure towering in front of us was the blue-rinsed hair. The woman's voice was as gruff as her exterior.

"Can I help you?" she inquired.

I was tongue-tied, but Lee managed to find the words. "We're looking for Robert Mallory."

"Moved out several months ago," she barked, backing away preliminary to shutting the door.

"Wait." Lee wedged her small body against the closing door. "Can you be more specific?"

"Well, let me see." The manager scratched her chin with a hand big enough to be a major-league catcher's mitt. "It was before Thanksgiving, I recollect that. And after Halloween."

"Are you sure?" Lee persisted.

"Oh yes, I don't know dates, but I do remember holidays. Yes, Bob was definitely here for Halloween."

"By any chance did he leave a forwarding address?" I asked hopefully.

The woman shook her huge head.

"No, he didn't even give any notice. One day he was here, the next he was gone." She frowned. "Not at all like Bob. He was always very dependable."

"How long did he live here?"

"He was here when I came," the manager said, "and I've been here seven years, come Valentine's Day."

"Do you know what he did for a living?" I asked.

The lady frowned again, this time at me. "I think I've said enough," she boomed, and started to close the door again.

"Do you have any idea where he might have gone?" Lee called to the disappearing giant. "It's really important we find him."

"Far as I know, Bob only had one friend." The door stopped one inch from the sill. "Name's Henry. Runs an antique store down on Seventh. Called the Copper Penny, I think. Check with him." The door clicked shut.

* * *

"Could you believe the size of that woman?" I asked Lee, once we were back out on the sidewalk.

"Yeah," she laughed. "I bet none of her tenants are ever late with the rent money."

"You got that right."

"But she did give us some useful information," Lee said. "Especially the lead about Henry."

"Yeah, the trail's not dead after all. But I think the time element's also interesting."

"Which one?" Lee laughed again, walking toward the car. "Halloween or Thanksgiving?"

I smiled. "The lady was really a character, all right." I opened the passenger door for Lee. She slid inside. I propped my elbows on the open door and leaned over her. "If what she says is true, Robert Mallory disappeared just about the time Ted Nichols turned up on Izzy's doorstep."

"You think there's a connection?" Lee asked, as I slammed the door. I walked around behind the car, opened the driver's door, and occupied my seat behind the steering wheel.

"I think it's a possibility," I said, belatedly answering her question.

"But Izzy would have recognized Mallory," Lee insisted. "Anyway, he described Nichols as a young man, and Mallory would be in his early fifties by now." She shook her head. "Izzy'd never be that far off base."

"No, no, you don't get it," I said. "I'm not saying that Mallory passed himself off as Nichols." I placed the key in the ignition. "I'm saying he could have gotten someone else to play the part."

"Why?" Lee asked, as the Cadillac spurted to life.

"That, my dear, is something I don't know," I answered, easing the car out into the traffic. "But maybe this Henry does."

* * *

The Copper Penny occupied a small storefront on Seventh Street, squeezed between a secondhand bookstore on one side and an upholstery shop on the other. The bell over the door announced our entry.

The interior was dim and cluttered with Victorian-era furniture. Tables, chairs, sofas with dirty-looking antimacassars, hutches, and highboys. Totally unappealing, if you asked me. I couldn't imagine anyone wanting these dark and dingy pieces in their homes. I certainly didn't.

A man emerged from the gloom, walking toward us from the back of the shop.

"May I help you with something?" he inquired, without inflection, without expectation, but with just the trace of an accent.

"Are you Henry?" Lee asked.

"Henri," he corrected, then gave a slight bow. "At your service."

Lee smiled. "We're looking for Robert Mallory," she said. "Do you know where he is?"

A sudden sadness enveloped Henri's face. He covered his eyes with his hand. His head moved up and down.

"Yes, I know," he said. Then his hand abruptly dropped from his face, and he glared angrily at Lee. "But why do you come here?"

"The manager at his old apartment building suggested that you might could help us find Mr. Mallory," Lee answered.

"Ah, yes." He smiled. "Edna, the queen of the harpies, I should have known." Henri dropped the smile. "But what is it you want?" he demanded.

"A friend, Mr. Mallory's former agent, Izzy Cohen, asked us to look him up," Lee answered. "Izzy sent him a gift." Lee fished in her purse and brought out the package, extending it toward Henri. "See?"

"I have never heard Robert" (he gave it the French pronunciation) "speak of this Izzy Cohen," Henri said. "But it is of no importance."

He turned and walked back into the gloom, Lee and I fast on his heels.

"You're wrong," Lee argued. "It's very important. We've come all the way from New York City. We must contact him."

Henri stopped and turned back toward Lee. "Madame, you misunderstand."

"Well, maybe you can enlighten me then."

"I only mean it is of no importance to Robert," he said sadly. "Not any more."

"What do you mean?" Lee persisted.

"Robert is dead," Henri said simply.

*　*　*

Five minutes later Lee and I were sitting inside Henri's tiny office, mugs of coffee in our hands. Henri sat opposite us, behind a cheap metal desk. Sheaves of paper covered the writing surface.

"Robert had AIDS," Henri said. "He didn't want anybody to know. In November, he moved into an AIDS hospice. He died there last week."

"Did you know he was a former actor?" Lee asked.

"*Oui*, I knew. But it was not something Robert talked about."

"How long had you known him?"

Henri smiled. "I met Robert shortly after I moved to Long Beach, right after I opened this store. That was about ten years ago. He just walked in one day, looking lost and helpless, like he didn't have a friend in the world."

"And did he?" I asked.

"Not really," Henri said. "Robert was a loner. He didn't mix well with people, didn't fit in. I found out later he had been in a mental hospital for several years, had only been out a few days when he came in here."

Henri pulled open the center drawer, lifted out a pack of cigarettes, shook one out, and stuck it in his mouth.

"Oh, excuse me," he said, "will it offend you if I smoke?"

"We're both trying to quit," Lee said. "But don't let that stop you."

He took the cigarette out of his mouth and tamped it back in the pack. "I know what it is to quit," he volunteered. "I have done so many times."

Lee and I both laughed, and Henri visibly relaxed, a smile touching his eyes. "Robert did not like the smoke, either," he said.

"If it's not being too personal," Lee said, "could you tell us how he contracted the disease?"

Henri interlaced his fingers and tapped gently against his

chin. "If it were only a simple matter of love, maybe it would be understandable," he said. "But Robert had a dependency on drugs. On cocaine, specifically. It is most likely he got the AIDS from shared needles."

Lee inquired softly, "Were you his lover?"

Henri grimaced. "I would have been, and gladly. But Robert was too committed to misery. He would not allow the possibility of happiness to enter his world."

"I don't understand," Lee said.

Henri smiled, shaking his head. "Neither did I," he answered. "Robert would never let me get close enough to help."

"He sounds like a most unappealing character," I said. "How did you ever become friends?"

Henri laughed. "I think Robert would have agreed with you, *monsieur*. But there was such a longing in Robert, such a need, I don't know, it just touched me, and made me love him."

Lee reached in her handbag and retrieved Izzy's package. "This is for Robert," she said. "What do you think we should do with it?"

"I cannot take it, madame. Robert's ashes are there on that mantel behind you." I glanced over my shoulder and spotted a large Grecian urn. Copper. "If you prefer, you may drop it in there. Perhaps that would be the right thing to do. Or you might choose to return it to the benefactor." Henri paused, then added solemnly, "Whatever you think best."

"I think Izzy would like it to rest with Robert," Lee said,

rising from her seat. She lifted the urn's lid, slipped the package through the opening, and replaced the covering.

Lee smiled. "Thank you, Henri," she said.

"But I have done nothing, madame," he objected.

"You were a friend to Robert, a good friend," Lee said. "And that's quite a lot. Tell me, did he die peacefully?"

Henri pushed his chair back from the desk and stood up. "No, madame, he did not." He lifted Lee's right hand to his cheek. "But that is not what you are asking." He dropped Lee's hand and smiled, tears shining in his eyes. "*Oui*, the end came easily. It was just the years leading up to it that did not, the days and nights of living death. Ah, poor Robert."

"Good-bye, Henri," said Lee. "And again, thank you."

"It is I who must thank you," he said. "I was unable to mourn for Robert until now. You have made that possible."

"How?" Lee asked.

"Because now I know that somebody else did care. He wasn't so alone after all."

* * *

"I feel like such a heel," Lee said, once we were back in the car, "intruding on that poor man's grief."

"We weren't intruding," I pointed out, "and he appreciated our visit."

"He thinks we cared about Robert." Lee unintentionally affected Henri's French pronunciation.

"Izzy cared," I suggested, "and we're Izzy's representatives. So, by extension, we do care. We weren't being phony. Anyway, we told him right up front why we had come."

Lee smiled. "I guess you're right."

I patted her hand. "Good girl," I said. "I don't want you getting maudlin on me. Anyway, I've got another title to add to my list."

"Quick, tell," Lee insisted, as she buckled her seatbelt.

"Marcia Muller's *Edwin of the Iron Shoes*."

Lee hooted. "The antique store did it."

"Well, yes, in a way," I admitted. "But I could just have easily thought of Lovejoy."

"Then why didn't you?" she teased.

"Maybe it's because we're in California and not England," I said. "More likely it's because *Edwin of the Iron Shoes* is not only a great mystery, it's a landmark in the genre. Marcia Muller broke the ground for all the hard-boiled women mystery writers who followed. And I think she's been unfairly overlooked for far too long. You always hear people crediting Grafton and Paretsky, but seldom a mention for Muller. I think it's an outrage." I started the engine. "But mostly I selected *Edwin of the Iron Shoes* because it is one of my all-time favorite mysteries."

"Mine, too," Lee chorused.

Sue and Sara, eat your hearts out!

CHAPTER 15

*R*ush-hour traffic is no laughing matter in Southern California. Drivers kill to protect a few freeway inches, maniacally determined not to let any other vehicle get a logistical advantage, eager to beat all comers at this ridiculous modern-day jousting match, risking smashed bumpers and cardiovascular trauma just to carve a few seconds off the homeward journey. Were Dante suddenly to return to twentieth-century America, the five P.M. weekday Basin inferno would surely qualify as his first circle of hell.

"We might as well forget stopping by the hotel," I said, gripping the steering wheel with both hands. "At this rate, we'll be lucky to get to Pasadena by midnight."

The Cadillac floundered landlocked on the Long Beach

Freeway. In the past half hour, our tortoiselike progress had barely covered three miles, a pace that would easily put us at the back of the pack in any halfway decent footrace. The mood I was in, for a good pair of Nikes, I'd chuck the car and walk.

"Kyle, we can't meet Alexander Paxton in these clothes," Lee wailed. "We've been in them all day. They've been soaked and dried out twice. We're nothing but a mass of wrinkles."

"I can't help it," I said irritably. "You're the one who set the meeting for seven." I looked at my watch, dimly visible in the late afternoon twilight. "It's almost six now, and we're not even to Alhambra."

On asphalt reflection, the side-trip to Long Beach had been ill-advised. Lee and I had simply miscalculated the time. We had left Toby Vickers shortly after one, leaving us a seemingly manageable schedule. But we had tarried too long at the restaurant, expended too much energy on the Amazon landlady, and shared too much sympathy with Henri. Now we were paying the price. But, considering what we learned about Robert Mallory, I felt it had been worth the effort.

"I can't greet a famous actor looking like this," Lee said.

"You look fine," I said perversely, well aware Lee felt exactly the opposite. "Anyway, if he's anything like the character he played on television, the guy won't notice anyone but himself."

Alexander Paxton was perhaps the only one of Izzy's clients I knew anything about, and that was because he had starred in "Brighton Blackie," a detective series that had first aired in the late fifties and early sixties, and had since enjoyed a long afterlife in rerun syndication. The character Paxton had portrayed—Sylvester "Blackie" Swanson—had been a foppish and effete intellectual, somewhat on the order of Lord Peter Wimsey. I had never particularly cared for the actor or his role, though I grudgingly conceded Paxton fit the part to perfection. No, what made me a die-hard fan of the show came more from the first-rate scripts, the authentic atmosphere, the inventive puzzles, and the superb supporting cast. Still, I couldn't deny I felt just the tiniest thrill of anticipation at the prospect of finally seeing him in person.

"And what kind words does Izzy have for Mr. Paxton?" I asked Lee, as the Cadillac inched forward, just nosing out the BMW on my left.

"He doesn't," Lee answered hotly. "Izzy calls him an overbearing, disagreeable snob."

I frowned. "Then why did Izzy want to bed him down?"

"He didn't. He says here the whole thing only happened because Lev had such a gigantic crush on Paxton that Izzy reluctantly went along with it." Lee laughed. "Izzy also claims that the main reason Alexander Paxton agreed to participate was that his ego was so huge."

"From what Izzy writes, Paxton must be a lot like the character he played in his TV show," I mused. "No wonder he did it so well."

"Was the character a real charmer, too?" Lee asked sarcastically.

I nodded. "If anything, even more irritating than the way Izzy describes Paxton," I said. "You never watched it?"

Lee shook her head. "I can't say that I did. I certainly don't remember it."

"It was a pretty terrific mystery series," I commented, "though not as good as 'Perry Mason' or 'Burke's Law.' The writing's really what made it work."

"I wonder what Paxton's been doing since the show went off the air?"

"I don't know," I answered. "But you won't have long to wonder. In less than an hour, you can ask him yourself."

"If he's willing to talk," Lee said.

"And if he's not a complete jerk," I modified.

"And if we ever get off this damn freeway," Lee added pointedly.

I grimaced. At the rate these lanes were moving, that last if loomed as the biggest one of all.

* * *

Needless to say, we did make it off the Long Beach Freeway. Finally. At precisely six thirty, the traffic clot miraculously dissolved and the L.A. arteries started flowing again. We even got to Alexander Paxton's house with five minutes to spare.

Did I say house? Buckingham Palace was more like it, with enough illumination to light up Yankee Stadium. Paxton's abode bore as much resemblance to the normal house as Rembrandt's *Night Watch* did to a union card.

"The place must have at least thirty rooms," I said, as I closed the car door behind Lee.

"I've always heard about conspicuous consumption," Lee commented, "but this is the first time I've seen it on such a grand scale."

A uniformed maid answered the bell and escorted us into a sitting room, just off the main entry hall. She excused herself, saying she would inform Mr. Paxton of our arrival, then closed the door behind her as she departed.

It was a small room, relatively speaking, no more than half a football field in width, with possibly an eighteen-foot ceiling. Paintings by the old masters dotted the walls, and I had a pretty good idea they weren't copies. In surroundings like this, nothing but originals would do. Several Oriental throw rugs rested comfortably against the polished mahogany floor. Lee and I tiptoed self-consciously around the colorful coverings and perched uncomfortably on a fragile-looking Queen Anne sofa.

"I didn't know that anybody actually lived like this," I whispered.

Lee nodded. "It'd be like living in a museum," she agreed. "I'd even be afraid to breathe around some of this stuff, let alone touch it."

Lee and I sat in mutual silence, too overwhelmed by the surroundings to speak. Alexander Paxton kept us waiting for five minutes, then made his grand entrance.

"You arrived two minutes early," he said, without any preliminary greeting. "I expect people to be on time, not early and not late. You're fortunate I'm not holding your lack of punctuality against you."

In tandem, we rose to our feet.

"And we, for our part," said Lee, with a saccharine sweetness that would have killed flies, "won't hold your lack of good manners against you, Mr. Paxton."

He harrumphed at Lee's comeback zinger, but said nothing. Lee then proceeded to explain the nature of our business, which gave me an opportunity to study the man who would, at least for me and perhaps for millions of other fans as well, forever be the one and only "Blackie" Swanson.

The years had not been kind to Alexander Paxton. He still maintained the same regal bearing and supercilious attitude of his television days, but his body was collapsing against the relentless onslaught of Father Time. I knew Paxton's true age to be somewhere around sixty-five, but the man looked more like eighty. His once elegant tan lay yellow against his skin, his signature pencil-thin moustache appeared as barely a waxy gray shadow on his upper lip, and his formerly tapered hands, now stiff with arthritis, shook constantly.

"I'm afraid I don't know what you're talking about," Paxton was saying to Lee. "I never did any such thing."

"But Izzy—"

"Izzy is mistaken. Or he's gone senile. I don't know which." Paxton straightened his back. "I simply know it's not true."

Lee glanced toward me. I shrugged.

"Mr. Paxton," she continued, "Izzy was concerned you might be blackmailed."

"Young woman, I can assure you I have never done anything that would warrant blackmail. I have lived an exemplary life, and I have nothing to hide. But I must warn you," Paxton said archly, "if you or Izzy persist in this slander, I will be forced to seek legal remedies."

"No such action will be needed, Mr. Paxton," Lee said hotly. "No one wishes to sully your saintly reputation."

"Alex, are you in here?" An elderly woman appeared in the doorway. "Oh, hello. I thought I heard voices." The lady smiled. "Alex, why didn't you tell me we had company?"

"They came to see me, Abby," Paxton answered abruptly. "And they're just leaving."

"Nonsense." She walked over to where we were standing. "My husband's manners are atrocious, aren't they, dear?" she said, addressing Lee. "I'm Abigail Paxton."

"I'm Lee Holland, and this is Kyle Malachi."

"Won't you sit down," Abigail said. "I don't know why my husband kept you standing."

Lee and I resumed our seats on the Queen Anne sofa, and Abigail sat across from us in a winged Chippendale. Paxton stubbornly remained standing.

Abigail Paxton was tiny, probably no more than four-feet-ten in height, and I doubted if ninety pounds would even tip her scales. But she possessed the residual grace of a once proud beauty. Age had long ago chased away the youth from her face, which bore the unmistakable tautness of too many cosmetic surgeries. But there was a vitality about her that belied her advanced years. Her green eyes sparkled with perpetual energy and excitement.

"Now what did you want to see my husband about?"

Lee answered, choosing her words with care. "A mutual friend asked us to pay our respects."

"Really?" Abigail asked, "and who would that be?"

"Isidore Cohen. You see—"

"Ah, Izzy." Abigail leaned back in her seat and laughed. "I haven't seen Izzy in years. But he was a delightful man." She leaned forward and whispered conspiratorially, "And he gave the most outrageous parties. How is he?"

"He's fine. We just saw him a few days ago." Lee reached into her bag. "He knew we were coming out to L.A., and he asked us if we'd deliver this to Mr. Paxton." Lee withdrew the wrapped package.

"Wonderful, I love presents," Abigail applauded. "What's the occasion? I know it's not Alex's birthday, and Izzy never was one to give Christmas gifts."

"I think it's just a keepsake," Lee answered, still cradling the package in her outstretched hand.

"Well, Alex," chastised Abigail, "aren't you going to accept Izzy's present?"

I could read the hostility in Alexander Paxton's eyes, but he walked over and almost snatched the present out of Lee's grasp.

"I guess you know that Izzy was Alex's agent," Abigail said, "but I bet you didn't know he was mine as well."

"No," we both said in chorus.

She nodded, smiling. "Yes, Alex may have starred in 'Brighton Blackie,' but I wrote the scripts."

"You're kidding," I gasped, "that's marvelous. I always thought those were the best story lines on television."

Abigail seemed genuinely pleased at my enthusiasm.

"I can't tell you how pleased I am to get to meet you," I said.

Abigail started to respond, but her husband cut her off. "Abby, are you forgetting our dinner party? We have guests arriving in less than thirty minutes."

"Oh my, yes." She stood up; Lee and I rose to our feet as well. "I must get dressed," she said. "But at my age, it's a lot easier than it used to be. I don't have to worry so much anymore about looking pretty."

She laughed, and so did we. Lee and I walked to the front door, Abigail between us. Alexander Paxton remained childishly behind.

"Thank you so much for the nice visit," said Abigail. "It's so good to see young people again. I'm afraid all our visitors nowadays are either as old as we are, or they're medical personnel."

Lee and I laughed again. Abigail had that effect, her good-natured humor was simply contagious. We thanked her for her hospitality.

"Do come again," she said, as we walked out on the steps. "And don't mind my husband. That's just his way." She waved a smile and closed the door.

"How in the world has she ever put up with him all these

years?" Lee demanded, as I held the passenger door open for her.

"I can't imagine," I said, "but she is a cutie."

"She is indeed," Lee agreed. I walked around the Cadillac and eased behind the wheel.

"I wonder how he's going to explain Izzy's little present?" Lee grinned maliciously.

"I don't know, and I don't care," I said, matching Lee's malice. "That's Mr. Alexander Paxton's problem, and he's more than welcome to it."

* * *

"I bet she's the one with the money," Lee said, as we headed toward downtown L.A. and the Bonaventure Hotel. After the rugged day we had put in, Lee and I had decided that our immediate agenda had to include a hot shower, a change of clothes, and a room-service meal. In that order.

"Definitely," I concurred. "Abigail's the one with the breeding. He just has the bad manners."

Lee giggled. "And can you get over the fact she wrote 'Brighton Blackie.' "

"After meeting her, I'm not surprised," I said. "I always felt those scripts were the best thing about the series, and now I know why."

"I think she probably even got him the part."

I nodded. "Or wrote the part specifically for him," I added. "The role certainly fits Alexander Paxton's personality. You can't tell me the producers would have selected him under any other circumstances."

Lee and I rode the rest of the way to our hotel in companionable silence. It was well after eight P.M. when, totally exhausted, we left the Cadillac in the parking garage, trudged to the elevators, and headed directly to our room. As I unlocked the door, the red message light on the phone blinked a welcome.

"You or me?" Lee asked.

"You," I answered. "More than likely, it's for you anyway."

Lee lifted the receiver and punched in the numbers for the hotel's message service. She listened for a minute, broke the connection, then dialed again.

"It's my service in New York," Lee said, cradling the phone between her shoulder and chin while she searched the writing desk for pen and paper. "They said it was urgent."

I sat on the king-size bed and awaited the outcome. It wasn't long in coming.

"Hello," Lee said. "This is Lee Holland. I had a message to call." Lee listened intently, then her face paled. "Oh no, I can't believe it," she moaned. "Is that all the information you have? I see. Yes, we'll fly back tomorrow. Thanks."

"What is it?" I demanded, as soon as she had replaced the receiver.

"Oh, Kyle," Lee cried, and there were tears in her eyes. "Izzy's dead."

* * *

Two hours later, after half a dozen phone calls, Lee had finally booked us two first-class tickets on a TWA flight leaving

LAX at ten A.M. Pacific Standard Time, and arriving at Kennedy at five fifty-five P.M. Eastern Standard Time. In between her efforts, she had wolfed down the patty melt, french fries, and chocolate milkshake I had ordered from room service using the house phone down the hall. Since first things came first, we had foregone the anticipated shower and change of clothes, but I knew neither of us would get through the night without something to eat.

"I guess we'll just have to wait until we get back to New York," Lee said, exhaustion slurring her words, "before we find out what happened."

"I have an idea," I said, chewing on my last fry. "Why don't I give Nolan a call, and see if he can find out anything for us." I pulled out my wallet and started sorting through the numerous pieces of paper I constantly stashed there, searching for Nolan's unlisted telephone number.

"Kyle, it's after one in the morning back there," Lee said. "Anyway, who's Nolan?"

"Nolan's my next-door neighbor. You've heard me talk about him."

"Of course," she said. "He's the one who collects your mail when you're out of town."

"That's right. And he's also the one who's an ex-cop and who just may be able to use his contacts to cut through some of that notorious bureaucratic red tape New York City is so famous for."

"He was in the NYPD?" Lee asked.

I nodded. "His last two years," I said. "Before that, he

was on the force in Chicago, or Detroit, or one of those big cities in the Midwest."

"Was he a detective?"

"Yes," I answered. "In homicide."

"Oh."

"Aha, success," I said, finally locating the correct notation, and waving it at Lee.

"You're sure he'll be willing to do this for you?"

"Nolan won't mind at all," I promised, picking up the phone. "He'll be glad to help. It'll make him feel useful." I punched in the number.

"I still can't believe Izzy's dead," Lee said, as I waited for the connection to Tipton. "He was so much alive when I saw him just a couple of days ago, and he sounded fine when I talked to him this morning."

"Yeah," I said. "It's hard for me to believe, too."

A silence suddenly loomed between us. I wondered if Lee was trying to repel the word that kept repeating itself over and over in my thoughts, but that neither of us had yet spoken aloud. I heard Nolan's sleepy voice on the other end of the phone line, but my mind still embraced that single word.

Such an ominous word, such an evil one, surely such an impossible one.

Murder.

CHAPTER 16

"Readers tired of constant doses
of blood and gore
will find a refreshing
change."

—Stokes Moran,
on Elizabeth Peters'
The Last Camel Died at Noon

"I hope you didn't leave that x-rated videotape in the room," I whispered to Lee as we stood at the hotel checkout desk.

She shook her head. "It's rolled up in a pair of pantyhose and stuffed all the way in the bottom of my suitcase," she whispered back.

Good, I thought. It'd be awfully embarrassing if that thing suddenly popped out. Too much explaining to have to do.

It was almost nine A.M. Once again, Lee and I had pushed the limits of our allotted time. We had planned to get up at six, but we had simply overslept. It had been after seven before we had finally roused ourselves, and then certain morning rituals conspired to occupy our attention. Those, er, activities had really put us in a bind. So to speak.

I looked once again at my watch and realized we were going to be cutting it close—driving to the airport, returning
the rental car, checking our luggage, finding our departure
gate—all with just a little more than an hour to go. I hoped
the fates would be on our side.

Lee accepted the receipt from the clerk, stuffing it and her
credit card back in her purse.

"Well, everything's taken care of," Lee said. "We're all
set."

"It's about time," I commented and waved to the porter
to follow us with our bags. I had earlier brought the car
around to the front entrance, a move which would, I hoped,
give us a little extra cushion of time.

I had just stashed the last piece of luggage in the trunk
when I heard a wild Texas yell. Looking up, I spotted Mike
Conover running toward us. My first thought—he's come
after his tape.

Breathless from his exertion, Conover joined Lee and me
at the side of the Cadillac.

"I was afraid I had missed you," he gasped. "I tried calling, but there was no answer. So I thought I'd take my
chances and just come on down."

"If you've come about—" I started, but Lee abruptly
stabbed me in the ribs with her elbow.

"What is it?" Lee asked quickly, effectively drowning out
my words.

He frantically gulped air. "Did you hear about Izzy?" he
wheezed.

"Yes," Lee answered solemnly. "We got word last night."

"Well, a friend of mine called me this morning from New York to let me know," Conover said. "First people I thought to let know was you. I'm glad I caught you."

Lee reached out and grasped Conover's hand. "Thank you very much, Mike. It was really very thoughtful of you to go to so much trouble."

"Think nothing of it," he said. "Izzy was very special to me. It's the least I could do."

Conover, seemingly content now that he'd delivered his message, offered nothing further, and Lee and I had no more words to add either.

"Well, I hate to break this up," I said, finally interrupting the awkward silence, "but we've got a plane to catch."

"Don't let me keep you," Conover said. "I just wanted to make sure you knew." He backed away, then stopped and asked, "Do you think there'll be a funeral, or a memorial service, or something?" His words seemed hesitant, tentative, almost shy.

"I don't know," Lee answered. "Izzy didn't have any relatives still around that I know about. Plus, he wasn't very religious and, I'm sure you know, he despised convention." She shrugged. "But he does have an awful lot of friends who I'm sure will want the opportunity to say a final good-bye. So, who knows? We'll just have to wait and see if he left any instructions."

Conover nodded throughout Lee's statement. "Well, let

me know, will you? Well, see ya." He waved, turned, and darted across the parking area.

"Why did you elbow me?" I demanded, as soon as Conover was out of earshot.

"I was not about to unpack my suitcase," Lee said irritably, "and expose to public view both my pantyhose and that tape. Besides," her tone softened, "he didn't come for that anyway."

"No, but we could have given it back to him and gotten it off our hands."

"We didn't have time," she reminded me.

I checked my watch. "You mean we don't have time. We've only got forty-five minutes, or we'll miss our flight. Come on, let's go."

"Don't worry, we'll make it," Lee said, opening the passenger door. "You'll see to that."

"How can you be so sure?" I asked sarcastically, climbing into the driver's seat.

"Because," Lee smiled, "you couldn't survive a minute longer in L.A. than you absolutely had to."

She was right about that. We made it to the airport with time to spare.

* * *

"What do we do now?" I asked, finally breaking the silence.

Lee had been unusually subdued for the past two hours, listening to music, pretending to read the flight magazines, napping. I recognized the external signs. I knew firsthand the gut-wrenching upheaval death always visits on the ones who are left behind. I lost both my parents before I turned twenty-one, but even so I could only imagine the emotional chaos churning beneath Lee's calm surface. Grief, despite all the self-help seminars and well-intentioned therapies, remains a private matter, unique to every individual.

Izzy Cohen had been an important person in Lee's life—her mentor, her adviser, her friend—and she needed time to come to terms with the loss. These past couple of hours had provided Lee with her first opportunity to really feel the hurt. Last night, the news of Izzy's death had been so sudden that a kind of protective numbness had enveloped her. This morning, our pace had been so rushed that any sorrow she might be experiencing just got shoved to the back of her mind. But isolated at thirty thousand feet, Lee had been unable to ward off the mourning any longer. Now, as we entered the last third of our cross-country flight, I felt Lee had privatized her feelings long enough.

"What?" Lee responded absently.

"I said, what do we do now?"

"About what?"

"About Izzy's assignment. Do we just end it, or do we go ahead and interview the last two men on the list?"

Lee shook her head. "Kyle, I don't think now is the time—"

I interrupted her words. "Now is precisely the time," I said. "Once we get home, we'll start to learn the details of Izzy's death, and we'll be faced with all sorts of distractions and interruptions. If we're going to pursue this thing, we have to decide it here and now."

"I don't know," she began, then her voice trailed off.

"Izzy wanted this done," I argued, "and, like it or not, we agreed to do it. For him. I for one think we should see it through."

"Maybe," she answered, "but then again maybe we've already satisfied Izzy's concern. We have uncovered absolutely no evidence of blackmail, and that's what Izzy was most worried about. I think we should perhaps let it go at that."

"Even if we find out that the missing tape is in some way connected to Izzy's death?" I asked. Neither of us had yet been able to speculate openly on the possibility of murder.

"Absolutely not!" Anger animated Lee's face. "If it turns out that Ted Nichols had anything at all to do with Izzy's death, then I'll make him wish he was never born."

I welcomed the return of Lee's characteristic spirit and fire. I knew if I could just keep her occupied with other matters, the next few days wouldn't be quite as difficult.

"The first thing I'll do when I get home," Lee announced, "is find out from Izzy's doctor exactly what happened."

"And for my part," I added, "I'll get with Nolan and see what his police contacts had to say."

"Good." Lee smiled for the first time since we boarded the plane. "Now we have a plan. Kyle, aren't you glad we got all this settled?"

I sighed. What's a future husband to do?

* * *

"Please stay in your seats until the plane comes to a complete stop," the flight attendant cautioned over the aircraft's intercom system as we taxied toward the terminal. "Thank you for flying TWA. Ground level temperature in New York is twelve degrees above zero, wind chill factor minus two. Have a nice day."

"Have a nice day, indeed," I muttered to Lee. "Who does she think we are, Eskimos?"

For the past two days, Lee and I had experienced a mild summer reprieve from winter's hoary sentence. Now we were about to face the teeth of the season once again.

"You sure you wouldn't like to turn around and head back to L.A.?" Lee teased. "We're both going to freeze in these clothes."

The airplane lurched to a halt, the hum of the engines ceased, and the overhead seat belt warning sign went dark. I unfastened my restraints and stood up, stretching my atrophied muscles. Lee reached under the seat in front of her and retrieved her purse.

"Fat lotta good it did us to lug coats all the way to California and back," I grumbled, "just to leave them packed away in our suitcases."

"Well, maybe it won't be too bad," Lee said. "You're wearing a sports coat, and I've got this silk jacket. Neither offers us much protection, but we might be able to make it all right if we don't have to stay outside too long at a time."

I scowled. "Yeah, that's easy to say. But wait till that wind hits us."

Lee smiled mockingly. "L.A.'s not looking too bad to you right now, is it?"

"L.A. was fine," I admitted. "There was nothing wrong with it that going back twenty years wouldn't fix."

I let Lee precede me toward the exit door. "Why stop at twenty?" she chided. "Why not make it thirty? Or forty?"

"I don't need to take it back that far," I smiled. "Walter Mosley already did it for me. His *Devil in a Blue Dress* nails L.A. in the forties."

Lee frowned. "What's that got to do with anything?" she asked, as we stepped out of the plane onto the enclosed ramp.

"Nothing, except that at least one good thing did come out of our trip to L.A."

"You've lost me," Lee admitted. "I have no earthly idea what you're talking about."

I grinned. "Here I've just told you the latest addition to my favorite mysteries list, and you weren't even paying attention."

She laughed. "You certainly picked a roundabout way to do it. Can't you do anything simple?"

"Where L.A. is concerned, there's no such thing as simple."

* * *

Lee and I rode in relative taxi warmth back to her apartment building, where she went upstairs to place a call to

Izzy's doctor, while I went downstairs to the parking garage to borrow her Land Rover for the drive out to Tipton and home.

And Bootsie.

The evening before, in addition to requesting Nolan's assistance in getting information on Izzy's death, I had also asked him if he'd mind collecting Bootsie at the kennel. Based on the flight schedule Lee had arranged, I knew that my arrival in Tipton would come well past Dr. Nancy's usual closing time, and I didn't want Bootsie to spend one minute longer than necessary in doggie purgatory. As the white lines of the highway pulled me closer and closer toward my destination, I pleasantly anticipated Bootsie's exuberant wet welcome. As the moment of reunion neared, I realized just how much I had missed my one-of-a-kind Irish setter.

And based on the reaction I got when she heard my voice at Nolan's door, Bootsie had missed me as well. Well, it wasn't that outrageous a response. After all, I told Nolan I'd pay for the lamp. It's not like there was any permanent damage. The door can easily be repainted, and Nolan's carpet probably needed a good shampoo anyway.

Ten minutes later, after getting Bootsie somewhat calmed down, I was finally ready to hear Nolan's report.

"Did you find out anything?" I asked, surreptitiously picking red dog hairs from the surface of Nolan's white cotton sofa, with Bootsie resting contentedly against my feet.

"Yep," he answered, sitting across from me in his rocker

recliner. "Seems like the New York cops are really confused over this one."

"What do you mean?"

"I'll get to that in a minute," he said. "First, let me fill you in on the details of the case." Nolan reached for his notebook, which lay on top of the coffee table, and flipped it open. "Years of habit," he explained. "If I don't write it down, it don't get remembered."

I laughed. "Once a cop, always a cop."

Nolan nodded his head vigorously. "You can sure say that again," he grinned.

"Let's see." He located the appropriate entry. "About nine o'clock last night, one of Izzy's neighbors took his dog for a walk and noticed that Izzy's front door was standing open. A few minutes later, on the return trip, when he found the door still open, the neighbor went to investigate. He found Izzy's body lying in a pool of blood just inside the front door, whereupon the neighbor immediately called the police." Nolan paused to clear his throat.

"First blues arrived on the scene," he continued, "at nine twenty-two. They in turn called for homicide and forensics. Mr. Cohen's personal physician was summoned. By ten P.M., the place was swarming with detectives, technicians, and medical personnel."

"Did they make any kind of preliminary finding?" I asked impatiently.

"The M.E. on the scene estimated the time of death at between seven and nine P.M. Since the body showed no signs of trauma or injury, the medical examiner gave a conditional ruling of death by natural causes, pending an autopsy, of course."

"Then there was no foul play," I interrupted.

"Just hold your horses," Nolan said irritably, "I'm getting to that. During the routine investigation of the premises, more blood was found in the elevator, in the third-floor hallway, and in what was later identified as Mr. Cohen's bedroom. All type O positive, same as the victim's."

"I don't understand," I said. "If there was no indication of—what did you call it?—trauma or injury to the body, where did all the blood come from?"

Nolan closed his notebook. "At first the doc said the blood probably was a result of a spontaneous nosebleed brought on by"—here Nolan flipped his notebook back open—"a ruptured thoracic aorta," he read, then he looked me in the eye. "But that diagnosis came before they found the bullet hole."

"Bullet hole?" I echoed.

"Yeah." Nolan laughed. "The cops found a bullet hole in Izzy's bedpost."

"You didn't tell me Izzy was shot!"

"I didn't because he wasn't. Remember I said there was no visible injury or trauma to the body," Nolan lectured. "Well, when you have a shooting victim, believe me, that's not something a trained pathologist is likely to miss."

"But what about the gun?"

"What gun?"

"You said—"

"I said the police found a bullet hole. I didn't say anything about a gun."

I frowned. "But you can't have a bullet hole without a gun."

Nolan laughed, shaking his head. "That's right. And you can't have a bullet hole without a bullet, either."

Nolan's cat-and-mouse routine was wearing thin. "Will you just tell me plain out what you're trying to say?"

"I said the cops found a bullet hole." Nolan paused for effect. "But I didn't say they found a bullet. Or a gun."

"You mean somebody removed the bullet and took it and the gun away with them," I said excitedly. "Then that means Izzy was definitely murdered. Without a doubt."

"No, no, no," Nolan objected. "You're jumping to unfounded conclusions." He stood up, walked over to his wet bar, and poured himself a Scotch and water. "Would you like anything?" he asked me. I said no thanks.

"Well, what other conclusion is there?" I demanded.

"I don't know," Nolan said, returning with his drink to the recliner. "But you always try to get all the evidence you can before you begin to form any theories. I learned that the hard way, with my first homicide case."

I let that reference pass. Nolan could fill me in on his infamous cases later. Right now I was only interested in Izzy's case.

I frowned. "Let me try to get all this straight," I said. "Izzy was found on the ground floor, lying in a pool of blood." Nolan nodded. "And blood was found in the elevator, the third-floor hallway, and in Izzy's bedroom."

"And on the bed," Nolan added.

"You didn't tell me that. And there was a bullet hole in the bedpost. But there was no bullet."

"That's right," Nolan agreed.

"Well then," I theorized, "if there was no bullet, then it naturally follows that somebody removed it."

Nolan shook his head. "Not necessarily."

"I'm confused," I admitted.

"Well, if you had let me finish my report before you started speculating, maybe you wouldn't be."

"You mean there's more?"

"As I said, there was a bullet hole in the bedpost. But there was also a bullet hole in the floor underneath the bed and in the outside wall of the house."

"How can that be?" I asked skeptically. "All caused by one bullet?"

"Best they can tell. All three holes are consistent with the trajectory of a single bullet."

"But that's impossible!" I exclaimed. "How can one bullet go through wood and mortar three times and still keep going?"

"Oh, there are guns that can send bullets right through steel," Nolan said, "and then some."

"But Izzy wasn't shot."

"That's right. Izzy wasn't shot."

"Well, what do the police make of all this?" I asked.

"They don't know what to make of it," Nolan admitted. "The bullet markings looked fresh, but they could have been there for weeks, even months. The cops don't know if the bullet holes are relevant to the current case or not. Right now, the police are going on the assumption that they are." He winked at me. "But you know what happens when you assume something, right?"

"Yeah," I answered absently. "It makes an ass out of both you and me."

He laughed. "Well, I can tell you from experience that cops don't like to be made asses of. They can't figure this one out, and that's got them mad."

"Good," I said. "Maybe that'll make them work harder."

"Oh, they're working harder, all right," Nolan confirmed. "They had a unit over there all day today going over every inch of that place, inside and outside, combing for that bullet, looking for anything that might explain what happened."

"What did they find?"

"I'm still waiting to hear," answered Nolan. "I probably won't get word until tomorrow morning, at which time hopefully I should also learn what came out of the autopsy."

"They've already done an autopsy?"

Nolan nodded. "This afternoon," he confirmed, then explained. "Whenever a celebrity's involved, the bureaucrats try to move as quickly as possible. Just in case there are any repercussions."

"Repercussions?"

"You know," Nolan laughed. "The mayor or governor takes an interest, the media gets involved, that kind of thing."

"Oh, I understand," I conceded. "They think it might turn out to be a high-profile case."

"Exactly."

I stood up, locking my right hand firmly around Bootsie's collar. "Thank you, Nolan." Unable to stand completely upright, I awkwardly guided Bootsie to the door. "You've been a big help." As soon as I spoke the words, I recognized the possibility of misinterpretation—as either a genuine appreciation to Nolan or a sarcastic admonition to Bootsie.

"Glad to do it," Nolan said, accurately reading my sentiment, and accompanying us out to the front steps. "Made me feel like I was back in harness once more."

"And I apologize again for the mess Bootsie made."

"Think nothing of it," he laughed. "House needed cleaning anyway."

"Well, I insist you send me a bill."

Nolan nodded. Bootsie was pulling impatiently against my grasp. I released her and watched her run toward my front yard.

"I guess Bootsie's telling me the visit is over," I said, then paused. "There's just one thing that doesn't make sense," I mentioned.

Nolan laughed. "Only one?"

I grinned. "Well, more than one, of course," I admitted. "But right now, just one that particularly has me stumped."

"What's that?" Nolan asked.

"If Izzy wasn't shot," I speculated, "then who was?"

Nolan didn't have an answer for that one, and neither did

I. Suddenly, all the compressed activity of the last few days fell like a sledgehammer against my back and shoulders. My knees and ankles buckled with fatigue. My body demanded immediate attention.

So, with my thoughts still in wild disarray, I walked slowly toward my front door. And a final end to this eternal day.

* * *

The following morning, in our routine run along the river, Bootsie found the body.

CHAPTER 17

"It's a
felonious assault
on the reader's funny bone,
a madcap mix
of
humor and homicide."
—Stokes Moran,
on Kathy Hogan Trocheck's
To Live and Die in Dixie

After taking a brief statement from me, the Tipton town police basically ignored my existence for the rest of the morning. Of course, with all my vast experience with dead bodies, I could have greatly assisted the authorities in their investigation. But then, they had no way of knowing that I've probably encountered more corpses than just about anyone on the face of the earth. From Victorian bodice-rippers to serial stalkers, from hard-boiled thrillers to locked-room puzzles, I've amassed a body count to rival Forest Lawn's. And as for my forensic skills, I learned everything I need to know from Patricia Cornwell and D.J. Donaldson. What better credentials could I have? Yet here I was, banished from the scene.

I alternated between standing uselessly outside in the blistering cold and sitting comfortably on my living-room sofa, watching the controlled activity through the large plate-glass windows that fronted on the river. For several hours, I maintained a constant vigil.

Over and over, I replayed the morning's events through my mind's eye video recorder—the urgency with which I'd rushed toward the water, my helpless slide into the river, my realization of what Bootsie had actually found. As soon as I'd pulled myself out of the muck, Bootsie and I ran to Nolan's house where he immediately covered me with warm blankets and phoned the police emergency number. Two uniformed officers responded within five minutes.

That had been approximately three hours ago. Nolan had elected to remain on the scene, but I had been shaking so badly he suggested I go home, get a shower, and change into some dry clothes. Which I did.

The ambulance attendants had removed the body some hour and forty-five minutes after the first unit had arrived. I had no idea what kept all those men gainfully occupied now that the body was gone. I had noticed nothing particularly informative about the crime scene the brief time I encountered it.

Tipton's chief of police had arrived shortly before the body was removed, and he and Nolan had been huddled together for the last half hour, whether from a willing partnership in the investigation or a more basic need for mutual warmth I couldn't tell. Finally, the two men broke apart, and Nolan headed toward my front door.

"Well," I demanded as soon as the door closed behind him, "what did you find out?"

Nolan shrugged out of his topcoat and shivered. "Do you have any coffee?"

"Just made a fresh pot," I answered, and led the way into my kitchen. "Have a seat, and I'll get you a cup."

Nolan sat on one of the barstools and clasped both hands around the brimming mug when I placed it in front of him. He took a cautious sip, then blew air against the rising steam.

"Now, give," I said.

Nolan set the mug gently down on the counter. "Guy was shot in the head," he said. "Bullet went clean through."

"How long had he been dead?"

"The coroner can't say for sure," Nolan answered. "Because of the freezing temperatures we've had the last couple of days, the time of death is no more than a guess."

"Well, what's the guess?"

"Coroner estimates somewhere between twenty-four and forty-eight hours. That's the best he can do."

"I see." I leaned back against the refrigerator and frowned. "Have they identified him yet?"

Nolan shook his head. "No, there was no identification on him," he responded, then added, "but you know who he is, don't you?"

That remark took me by surprise. "What do you mean?" I retorted. "How would I know a dead man I've never seen before?"

"I don't know, but I learned a long time ago there's no such thing as coincidence." He picked up his coffee and took a fresh sip. The steam wasn't quite so prominent this time. He continued, "Night before last, a friend of yours dies under what can only be called mysterious circumstances. Then this morning, you stumble over a corpse almost in your own backyard. My experienced cop's nose tells me something smells. Come on, you can tell me."

I nodded. "All right," I said, "but remember, this is still just supposition on my part. I have no proof," I protested.

"Yeah, yeah," Nolan said impatiently, "just spit it out."

"I think the dead man is Ted Nichols," I said. "I got a fairly good look at his face when I fell on top of him, and he looked like Lev Levin."

"Who?" Nolan demanded.

I then spent the next half hour filling Nolan in on both Izzy's story and my recent activities on Izzy's behalf. When I had finished, he asked, "So why do you think this Ted Nichols, if that's who it was, turned up here? And dead to boot?"

"My first thought was that he heard I was looking for him and came looking for me."

Nolan nodded in agreement. "That makes sense."

"It makes sense if he was killed here," I pointed out. "Not if he was killed in Izzy's townhouse."

"That's right. If he was shot there, he certainly couldn't have gotten all the way out here."

I nodded, then added, "Not on his own, that is."

"You mean you think somebody killed him in New York and then went to all the trouble to transport him some forty or fifty miles just to dump him in a Connecticut river right at the spot where you'd be sure to find him and perhaps guess his identity?" Nolan summarized incredulously. "I don't think so." He shook his head. "That doesn't make a lick of sense."

I agreed. "No, it doesn't," I said. "But that's the only way to explain the bullet hole in Izzy's bedroom." I stopped. "It's not likely there'd be a third body lying around someplace." I paused. "Unless . . . "

"Unless what?" Nolan instantly seized on the inflected word.

I shook my head. "I want you to check on something for me," I said. I gave him the gist of what I wanted.

"How long will it take you to find out?" I asked.

"I don't know," he answered. "Maybe a day or two."

"Okay," I said. "In the meantime, I'm going back into Manhattan and discuss all this with Lee. Will you keep Boot-sie for me?" After last night, I knew what an imposition that request conveyed. But good samaritan that he is, Nolan readily agreed.

"And you'll also get Izzy's autopsy results," I added, "as well as the latest update on the investigation?"

Nolan nodded his assent. "But you ought to tell the police what you suspect."

"I can't do that," I said. "What if I'm wrong? I have absolutely no proof that the dead man is Ted Nichols. It's all just a hunch right now," I said, then turned urgently toward

Nolan. "And promise me you won't say anything, either," I pleaded, "not until we're sure."

"All right," he agreed, "I'll keep quiet for a couple of days but after that, if I see the cops are wasting a lot of effort on the case and coming up with nothing, then I'll have to share this information with them—right or wrong," he concluded.

"Good," I said. "A couple of days should be plenty of time." I smiled and slapped Nolan on the back. "And maybe if we're lucky, we might just be able to present both the New York and Tipton police with a solved case."

* * *

"Wait a minute," Lee said. "You've lost me. You mean to say that you think the dead body you discovered this morning is Ted Nichols."

I nodded. "Actually, Bootsie found the body. But yes, that's exactly what I'm saying."

It was now early evening, and Lee and I were seated at her kitchen table, sharing a pot of coffee. I had not been able to get away from Tipton as quickly as I had hoped and, when I finally had departed, the traffic into the city had been monstrous. But I knew a few hours delay would not be that critical, not at this juncture at least.

"Okay, just for argument's sake, let's say you're right," Lee allowed, "that the dead man is Ted Nichols. Where does that get us?"

"What do you mean?"

"Ted Nichols, dead or alive, doesn't help us figure out what happened to Izzy, does it?"

"Maybe not," I conceded, then added, "then again, maybe it does."

Lee frowned. "Kyle, you're talking in riddles. None of this makes any sense."

"That's what Nolan said."

"Kyle, you're driving me crazy." Lee pushed back the kitchen chair and stood up. "Let's drop it for now. Take me out to eat. I'm hungry."

* * *

Over salad at Tatou, Lee filled me in on how her day had gone.

That morning she had talked with Dr. Martin Fisher, Izzy's personal physician, who had assured her that, as far as he could tell, Izzy had died of natural causes. In the afternoon, Izzy's attorney had called with the bombshell that Izzy had named Lee the executor of his estate. The attorney further alerted her that she would be receiving, by special messenger, some legal documents later in the day. Those had arrived just minutes ahead of me, and she had not yet had time to look them over.

"I plan to review them tonight," Lee said, munching on a radish. "I expect that his will's in there, along with burial instructions, insurance policies, and the like."

"Did Izzy leave much of an estate?"

"I don't know. I'm pretty sure he owned the brownstone, but aside from that, I don't have the vaguest idea. That's why I have to go through all the documents. I intend to do this job right."

"Well, Izzy certainly chose well," I said, reaching my hand across the table and touching her fingers. "His affairs couldn't be in better hands."

She smiled, then wiped away a tear. "Thank you, Kyle," she whispered.

"Did the attorney tell you anything about the police investigation?" I asked.

"No, not a thing."

"Then I guess we'll have to wait to hear from Nolan on that."

"Dr. Fisher did say he'd call with the autopsy results, as soon as he got word."

I frowned. "According to Nolan, the autopsy was scheduled for this afternoon. I wonder why he hasn't already called."

"Maybe the report's not yet ready," Lee answered. "You know how long it takes to make some people sit down and get the job done."

I can usually recognize a dig when I hear one, and, believe me, I definitely heard one in Lee's words.

"I'll have you know," I stated, between mouthfuls of lettuce, "that this afternoon I went through my review files and identified the hundred best ones for the book."

Lee's mouth dropped open. "I don't believe it!" she exclaimed.

"Well, don't be so shocked," I teased, "it's not quite the herculean task it sounds."

"What do you mean?"

"For years, I've filed my reviews under three categories—good, bad, and indifferent. So I just pulled out the good file, discovered it contained one hundred and seventy-eight reviews, removed any that featured a particular author more than once, and ended up with a grand total of a hundred and three. Then it was a cinch to pare those three off the top. And voilà, I had my hundred. As easy as that."

Lee's face still registered shock. "I'm impressed regardless," she said, chewing on a cracker. "But let me just ask you this. When you say good reviews, are you referring to the quality of the books or are you talking about the merit of the reviews?"

"The merit of the reviews, of course," I answered, "though the majority certainly are favorable to the books. As you know, I rarely give harsh assessments. My feeling has always been that with so many outstanding mysteries available for review, why waste my time telling people what not to read. No, in my philosophy, bad books just don't get mentioned at all."

"So," she concluded, totally ignoring my didactic aside, "the book's done."

"Not exactly," I said. "I still haven't finished my ten favorites list, though in going through the hundred reviews, I did come up with another title for my list."

"Oh, really," Lee said, leaning back to allow the waiter to

remove her plate, "and which one gets the lucky nod this time?"

"Carolyn G. Hart's *A Little Class on Murder*," I said, with a touch of acid in my voice. "It's a mystery lover's mystery, and one of the most enjoyable reading experiences I've ever had." I set down my fork. "Why are you being so snide?" I demanded.

"You're taking too long with this list, agonizing over it like it's the Bill of Rights or something." She smiled, somewhat taking the sting out of her words. "You've got other lists to complete. Why spend so much time on this particular one?"

"Because it's the most important. The subgenre lists are a piece of cake. I've already knocked most of those out, and I didn't worry about sticking to ten. I came up with seven favorite Christmas mysteries, and twelve ecclesiastical ones, in no time at all."

"Then why all the effort over the all-time favorites list?" she asked seriously. "I don't understand."

"It's hard to explain," I answered. "Selecting ten all-time favorites is a very exclusionary thing. In effect, I'm saying that all the hundreds and thousands of books that I'm not including just somehow missed the mark. And that's not true. Next year, even next month, I might have a totally different ten favorites list. I hate the whole concept."

"Then just forget it," Lee said. "It's not worth making yourself sick over."

I shook my head. "You don't understand. Even though I hate it, the process is making me define something in myself, something I had always chosen to avoid. It's forcing me to go out on a limb, to take a stand." I shrugged. "I can't explain it any better than that, I just know that's how it is."

"What you can't explain, at least to my satisfaction," Lee said archly, "is your insistent inclusion of Agatha Christie's *Curtain*. I'm just afraid that having that title on your list will demean your reputation."

"Nonsense. What is it you have against *Curtain*, anyway? The book was written at the height of Christie's powers, it details the death of Poirot, and it's got one of her most intriguing plots. In fact . . . " my voice trailed off.

"In fact, what?" she goaded.

"Nothing," I answered. "I was just reminded of something else."

"What?"

"It's not important," I said, pushing back my chair. "Are we ready to go?"

"My, you certainly change directions fast," Lee complained, rising to her feet as well. "Why the big hurry?"

I threw four twenties down on the table and took Lee by the arm, guiding her through the maze of tables.

"What's the big hurry?" she demanded.

"You've got documents to read," I said, "and I've got a trap to set."

"A trap?" she questioned. "A trap for what?"

"If we're lucky," I answered, "it'll be a trap to catch a killer."

CHAPTER 18

*"The joy
in reading this author
is in giving
yourself over wholeheartedly
to a zany
upside-down inside-out
mix of storytelling."*

—Stokes Moran,
on Charlotte MacLeod's *An Owl Too Many*

"Means, motive, opportunity," I mumbled.

Lee looked up from her reading. "What did you say?" she asked.

"Nothing," I answered.

I stood at Lee's living room window, looking down at the city. Snow had started to fall during our cab ride back from Tatou, and during the past two hours the flakes had grown in both size and density. A white downy quilt now covered the black asphalt of the surface streets, and the glistening white powder nestled like a shroud on the limbs of the trees in the curbside planters. The sudden metamorphosis of this most frenetic of cities into a pristine pastoral mosaic presented to me a vista of such peace, such clarity, and such precision that I envied its calm certainty and wished a simple thing like snowfall could transform my jumbled thoughts as easily.

Means, motive, opportunity. Those were the classic keys, the passwords, the open sesames to all the storybook mysteries. Every great fictional detective—from Sam Spade to Jane Marple, from Lew Archer to Kinsey Millhone, from Nick and Nora to Koko and Yum Yum—always identified these three elements well ahead of the final page. Just this once, why couldn't I do it too?

Maybe, just maybe . . .

I had a hunch, an intuition, a vague notion. Images fluttered through my brain—untested, not fully formed, but suggesting certain possibilities. Was this the magical process? Did solutions evolve only through a confused mixture of trial and error? Did truth finally emerge, not as a sudden earth-shattering revelation, but just from the rather mundane sifting of information?

"Kyle, guess what?" Lee said excitedly. "Izzy's willed his brownstone to an AIDS organization and directs that it be turned into a hospice which will be financed by the income from his investments. Wasn't that a wonderful thing for Izzy to do?"

"Yeah, sure," I answered, turning away from the window.

"Well, don't fall all over yourself with enthusiasm," she chided.

"I'm sorry, Lee." I walked over behind where she was sitting on the sofa, leaned down, and planted a kiss on the top of her head. "You're right. It is wonderful."

Lee grabbed my hand. "What is it, Kyle?" she asked. "You've been distracted ever since we left the restaurant."

"I don't know. I feel I ought to be able to solve this thing," I said, walking around the far end of the couch. "I've got a nagging—ouch!" I slammed my shin against something hard, stumbled, and almost fell.

"Kyle, I'm sorry." Lee jumped to her feet. "Did you hurt yourself?"

I shook my head. "No, I'm all right," I said, then kicked the suitcase in frustration.

"When I got in from L.A.," Lee explained, "I was so pre-occupied with finding out about Izzy that I never bothered to unpack. I meant to put that bag away before now, but, to tell you the truth, I simply forgot about it." She slid the luggage across the carpet, opened the closet door, and shoved it inside. "At least now it'll be out of harm's way," she said. "Now what were you saying?"

I squatted on the edge of the sofa. "I just feel," I admitted, "that I ought to be able to put this whole thing together."

Lee frowned. "Which thing are you talking about—Izzy's death, the murder of Ted Nichols, or the missing tape?"

"All of it," I responded adamantly. "I think that somehow it's all connected."

"Then you don't see these as three separate events?"

"Do you?" I asked skeptically.

"Well, we still haven't heard the results from Izzy's autopsy," Lee pointed out, "and you don't know for a fact that the body you discovered is actually Ted Nichols. And," she concluded, "there are two men on Izzy's list we haven't yet interviewed."

"I know." I pinched the bridge of my nose. "But I still can't help feeling that we've probably already got the information that would tell us who's responsible if we could only put it together in the right way."

"You mean information from our interviews?"

I nodded. "This whole thing started with that missing videotape," I acknowledged. "Somewhere, in all our bumbling efforts, somebody told us something important." I stood up. "I can feel it in my gut." I punched my abdomen. "But I guess I'm just too stupid to know what it is."

"Oh, no, you're not stupid," Lee disputed. "You're a reader. In fact, you're one of the all-time great readers of mystery fiction."

I scowled. "What does that have to do with anything?"

She smiled. "Doesn't there usually come a point in your reading where you become convinced you've got the puzzle figured out? Well ahead of the detective?"

I nodded. "Oh, sure," I answered. "Every reader does."

"Well, approach this problem as if it were just another mystery novel you're reading for review."

"But I'm not always right."

"Don't worry about that right now," Lee said. "Use the deductive abilities you possess as a reader and see what you come up with."

I smiled. "What the hell," I said. "I'll give it a try. After all, what do I have to lose? And anyway, what's the worst thing that could happen even if I'm wrong?"

Lee and I frowned in unison. Perhaps a wiser man would have left that last question unasked.

* * *

I couldn't sleep. I stared at the darkened ceiling, conscious of the rumbling heating unit, the ticking nightstand clock, the distant street noises, and Lee's light breathing, careful not to match my body movements to my mental gymnastics for fear I would wake her. I felt constricted, asthmatic, claustrophobic.

I rolled cautiously to the edge of the mattress and eased my body down to the floor. I knelt for a moment beside the bed, letting my eyes acquire as much night vision as possible. Then I rose to my feet and tiptoed silently toward what I hoped was the bedroom door.

The light snapped on. Startled, I swiveled around.

"What do you think you're doing?" Lee asked, her words somewhat slurred.

"I couldn't sleep," I confessed. "I was trying not to disturb you."

"What time is it?"

I glanced at the clock. "Three fifteen," I answered softly. "Just go back to sleep." Standing naked in the light made me feel vulnerable. I reached for my pants.

"Where were you going?" Lee's enunciation was growing

in precision. I knew the longer this conversation continued, the more wakeful she would become.

"I thought I'd find something to read," I answered hurriedly.

"There're some mystery novels on top of the dresser." She waved in the direction of her vanity. "I think some Simon Bretts and some Earl Emersons."

"Fine," I said, walking toward the books. "Now turn out the light and go back to sleep."

"You've got to see what you're doing," Lee protested.

I picked up the top book on the stack. "I've got it," I said. "Now turn out the light."

Lee squinted. "That's a Mac Fontana. I prefer the Thomas Blacks," she said drowsily.

"Fine." I walked over to Lee's side of the bed and switched off the lamp. The room returned to welcome darkness. I leaned down and nuzzled a kiss against Lee's left ear. "Now go to sleep," I ordered. She murmured something unintelligible, already halfway back to dreamland. I walked quietly out of the room.

Carefully feeling my way through the darkness, I waited until I was in the kitchen before turning on any lights.

I looked down at the book in my hand. Earl Emerson's *Morons and Madmen*. I hadn't really wanted to read; that had merely been a convenient excuse to get Lee back to sleep. I looked at the book again.

No, I thought, I didn't want to read. I decided I'd watch a movie instead.

* * *

"What time did you come back to bed?" Lee asked, as she stumbled into the kitchen.

"I didn't," I admitted, forking the bacon out of the frying pan.

"You didn't get any sleep?"

"Not a wink." I cracked four eggs into a mixing bowl, added a little milk, and whipped them to a frenzy.

"Then why are you so chipper?" she demanded, reaching for the coffeepot. "Was it my imagination, or did I hear you whistling a few minutes ago?"

"You know I can't carry a tune." But Lee was right. I had been whistling, not even aware I had been doing it, until it finally echoed back in my ears.

"Uh huh." She reached around me for the milk carton. "And this is the first time I've ever known you to make breakfast."

"I was hungry," I said simply.

Lee carried her mug to the table. "Okay, enough of this Ozzie and Harriet routine. What gives?"

I divided the scrambled eggs onto two plates, added strips of bacon and slices of toast, and carried the food over to the table.

"What do you mean?" I asked innocently.

Lee glared at me. "Last night you were a muddled mess, dejected and despondent. But this morning, well, you're like an entirely new person." She picked up a salt shaker and sprinkled salt over her eggs. "Now, it doesn't take an Einstein to see the difference."

"Okay," I conceded. "Maybe you're right."

Lee laughed. "I know I'm right," she barked. "But what I'm trying to find out is why?"

The phone rang. Lee slid her chair toward the counter and reached for the kitchen extension.

"Hello," she said, paused, then handed me the receiver. "It's for you," she added unnecessarily.

It was Nolan.

"Somebody's sure calling awfully early," Lee grumbled. "It's not even eight o'clock."

I listened to Nolan's report without comment, thanked him, then handed the phone back to Lee. She replaced it on the cradle.

"What was that all about?" she demanded.

"Just Nolan."

"And?"

"He was just sharing some information with me," I answered.

"About what?" she insisted. "This case?"

I smeared some strawberry jam on a piece of toast and crumbled bacon over it. "I'll fill you in later," I promised.

"No!" Lee slammed her fork down on the table. "I'm tired of this coy little act you're pulling. I always hate it in a mystery novel when the author keeps vital facts from the reader, and I'll be damned if I'm going to let you get away with it."

"Okay, okay," I laughed. "Don't get so upset."

"Then tell me what's going on."

"Yesterday I asked Nolan to check on a couple of things for me, and he was just calling in with the results."

Lee's frown intensified. "That's not an answer."

"All right," I said, growing more serious. "I asked Nolan to find out how Lev died."

Lee stared. "Lev?" she echoed incredulously. "What's Lev got to do with all this?"

"As it turns out, quite a lot."

"But Lev died five years ago from AIDS. We both know that."

"Do we?" I pushed back my chair, stood up, and carried my plate over to the sink.

"Yes, we do. Don't we?"

I shook my head, turned, and faced her. "Lev had AIDS, there's no doubt about that," I said. "But that's not what killed him."

"No?" Lee's tone had now grown considerably softer.

"No," I said. "All Izzy told us was that Lev died two days after finishing the album and videotape. But he didn't tell us how he died."

"Well?" The impatient tone had returned to Lee's voice.

I prolonged the moment, letting the drama build. "Lev committed suicide," I said finally. "He shot himself in the head."

C H A P T E R   1 9

"When challenging
anything this fraught with peril,
not losing
is nearly the same thing
as winning."

—Stokes Moran,
on William L. DeAndrea's *Killed on the Rocks*

"Then that explains the bullet hole, doesn't it?" Lee concluded.

"Possibly," I demurred.

Lee gave me an assessing look. "You've solved it, haven't you?"

"I think so," I answered.

We still sat at the kitchen table, lingering over second cups of coffee.

"Well," Lee demanded, when I offered no further explanation, "aren't you going to let me in on it?"

I nodded. "I'll be happy to share my theory with you," I agreed, stressing the word *theory*. "But first, did you come across any instructions from Izzy about his burial arrangements?"

"Yes. He's to be cremated, and he absolutely refuses to have a funeral."

"I see." I took my empty cup over to the sink. "Did he also rule out a memorial service?" I asked cautiously.

Lee shook her head. "No, he never addressed that subject."

I scurried back to my chair. "Good," I said. "That's what I needed to hear."

"Why?" Lee asked, puzzled.

"I want us to have a memorial service for Izzy," I explained, "and I want you to invite just the men on Izzy's list."

"The five we interviewed?"

"No," I answered. "Not just them, but also the two still left to go. I want all seven present."

Lee laughed. "That's going to be a little hard to arrange," Lee objected. "Unless you're planning to hold the memorial service in Los Angeles."

"No," I said. "It's going to take place in Izzy's brownstone."

Lee shook her head skeptically. "Then I don't think you're going to have a full house," she warned. "Those men didn't strike me as the kind who'd fork out big bucks for a plane ticket just to say good-bye to Izzy."

"Mike Conover indicated he might," I said.

"Then he'd probably be the only one. Kyle, don't you remember? Those men didn't seem to generate a whole lot of warmth toward Izzy."

I frowned. "Yeah, you're right," I admitted. "So how about if we offered to pay for their tickets?"

"Kyle, are you out of your mind? Do you have any idea how expensive that would be?"

"Don't we still have some of Izzy's ten thousand dollars left?" I reminded her. "We certainly didn't spend it all."

Lee nodded. "As a matter of fact, after the bills are paid, there'll probably be five or six thousand we won't need."

"Then that leftover money should cover the cost of the airline tickets." I tugged on her arm. "Shouldn't it?"

"Not for five first-class round-trip seats, it wouldn't," Lee said.

"Why first class?"

"Kyle, these are all famous actors who I'm sure will expect to fly first class."

"Well this time," I suggested, "make 'em fly coach. We can afford that, can't we?"

Lee laughed. "Oh, yes. No doubt about it." She stood up and walked over to the counter, where she filled her coffee cup with tap water and set it in the sink. "But why should we throw the money away like that?"

"Don't you think Izzy would want us to nail this guy? And the only way we're ever going to do that is to get them all in the same place at the same time. What better use for the money? Izzy would have wanted us to do it."

Lee laughed. "I don't know if I'd go that far," she cautioned. "But you're right. Izzy gave us that money with the clear objective of finding out what was going on. And if this memorial service accomplishes that, I think his money would have been well spent."

"Thank you." I swept Lee up in my arms and swung her off the floor. "How fast can you set it up?"

"I don't know," she said, somewhat breathlessly, once she had regained her footing. "I can make the calls this morning." She frowned. "The invitation itself shouldn't make anyone suspicious, but what do I say when they ask why we're willing to pay for their transportation?"

"Just say it was in Izzy's will."

"Kyle! I can't do that."

"Why not? It's not exactly a lie."

"No, that's going too far. I'll just say it's what Izzy wanted. I can live with that."

"Good." I turned on the hot-water tap and reached for the Dawn. "I'll wash up these dishes while you make the calls."

"I can't start calling yet. There's a three-hour time difference. It's not even daylight out there in Los Angeles yet."

"Then call the two men who are, I hope, still here in New York," I directed.

"You are eager," she said. "But before I make any calls, we still have to decide on a time, remember?"

"This afternoon."

"Kyle, be serious."

"Tomorrow."

"The earliest reasonable time," Lee insisted, "would be day after tomorrow."

"Fine," I answered. "That's it, then. Ten A.M., day after tomorrow."

"Ten A.M.?" Lee objected. "Don't you think either late afternoon or early evening would be a little bit more convenient?"

"I don't care about their convenience," I said, easing a stack of dirty plates into the hot and soapy water. "I'm just concerned about their presence."

"I wasn't talking about their convenience," Lee answered. "I was thinking about mine."

"Don't you see the irony in all this?" I lifted suds-soaked hands out of the water and wrapped them around her waist.

"What do you mean?" she asked, playfully resisting my embrace.

"We turned the tradition upside down," I answered, holding her tight. "Don't you see what we've done? Normally in murder mysteries, first comes the killing, then the suspect interviews, and finally the solution. But we had already interviewed the suspects by the time the killing took place. I don't think that's ever happened before."

"Hooray for us," she deadpanned. "I'll alert *The Guinness Book of World Records*."

"You pull this off," I promised, kissing her on the tip of the nose, "and I'll spend the rest of my days helping you set new records."

She smiled seductively. "Starting now?" she asked.

I nodded.

"Then ten A.M. it is," she said, grabbing my hand.

I never quite made it back to the dishes.

* * *

"I'm going to drive up to Tipton for the afternoon," I said an hour later, fastening the top button of my shirt. "Take Bootsie off Nolan's hands for a while, check the house, and perhaps even see if the Tipton police have come up with anything new."

"You'll be back tonight?" Lee crawled to the foot of the bed, the sheet wrapped around her.

I smiled. "Definitely," I said, bending down to kiss her. "But don't forget. You've got a lot of phone calls to make."

"I remember," she confirmed. "By the way, are you going to share your suspicions with the Connecticut cops?"

"I'm going to talk to Nolan first," I answered. "See what else he may have learned."

"Izzy's autopsy results should be in by now," Lee said. "I think I'll give Dr. Fisher a call to see if he's heard anything."

"Good idea," I approved. "Just in case Nolan's sources haven't come through."

Lee rolled off the bed and, sweeping the trailing sheet in her arms, followed me to the front door.

"What if the autopsy disproves your theory?" During our recent acrobatics, in a moment of easy camaraderie, I had incautiously shared all. What can I say? Lee has that effect on me.

"Then I suppose I'll be back to square one," I admitted frankly, then added, "if the autopsy proves me wrong, that is."

Fortunately, it didn't. Nolan had the results by the time I arrived in Tipton. Izzy died of natural causes, just as I'd assumed.

"It was exactly as I told you the other night," Nolan said.

"It was an—" Nolan reached for his notebook. "I don't know why I have such trouble remembering that diagnosis."

"Ruptured thoracic aorta," I supplied.

Nolan smiled. "Yeah, that's it." He found the proper notation. "Brought on by a history of hypertension," he completed the official finding.

Cold air flooded into Nolan's house. We were standing in his open doorway, so that I could keep a watchful eye on Bootsie. The poor man started to shiver. I whistled to Bootsie, and she came bounding toward the door.

"Have the police identified the body from the river yet?" I asked, closing the door after Bootsie's manic entrance.

"No," he answered. "I checked with them this morning. His fingerprints don't appear to be on file anywhere. Nothing came up on the FBI computers. I don't know how much longer I can wait without telling them who he might be."

"Then go ahead," I advised. "It'd be nice to have confirmation of his identity before I make a complete fool of myself."

"What do you mean?" Nolan asked, as he once again occupied his recliner.

I spent the next few minutes outlining my proposed solution to the case. After I finished, Nolan commented, "It sounds pretty good to me."

Taking that modest response as the closest I would probably come to an official police endorsement, I said good-bye, removing Bootsie from Nolan's immediate vicinity for a couple of hours. Leaving Bootsie happily occupied in the backyard, I spent the rest of the afternoon ensconced in my own living room, catching up on my correspondence, a singular pleasure recent events had also banished from my life.

At five P.M., I returned Bootsie to Nolan's care and drove back toward Manhattan. In less than forty hours, I'd know whether I was the real-life counterpart of Philo Vance or a possible defendant in a slander suit. I fervently hoped for the former.

* * *

"Great news," Lee said, as soon as I walked into the kitchen where she was busy making dinner. "Everybody I talked to has agreed to come."

"That's wonderful," I agreed, sniffing the homey aromas. "What's cooking?"

"Hungarian goulash," she said. "Now, leave that alone." She slapped my hand as I lifted the saucepan cover. "There's just one little problem," she added.

"What's that?"

"I still haven't been able to reach Max Morgan. He's been out all day showing properties. I left several messages for him to call me as soon as he gets back."

"So, what's the problem?"

"You know how adamant he was when we talked with him," Lee reminded me, "and remember, he even refused Izzy's gift. Now, I can't believe that even when he's out showing houses, he doesn't occasionally check with his office. He's bound to have gotten at least one of my messages by now. I'm afraid he's intentionally avoiding me."

"Let's not worry about that now," I said. "Boy, that sure does smell good."

After dinner, Lee started fretting about Max Morgan again.

"Look, why don't you just call him again?" I suggested. "Maybe this time you'll get him on the line."

"Everyone else was so easy," she said. "Why does he have to be so difficult?"

"He may not even be aware he's being a problem. Things are not always what they seem."

"You can say that again," Lee said, punching in Morgan's number on the telephone keypad.

"Last night," I continued, "I thought this was the most complicated situation I'd ever encountered. But when you get right down to it, it's a pretty simple and straightforward affair."

Lee nodded. "It's ringing," she said.

"It all boils down to just one thing," I said. "Motive. Once I understood that, the rest was easy."

"Yes, I'd like to speak to Max Morgan," Lee said. "Yes, I'll hold."

"But last night, when I was really wrestling with the puzzle," I said as she continued to hold, "I was reminded of one of the most complex novels I've ever read. And the more I thought about it, the more I realized it's one of my all-time favorites."

"Oh, here we go again," Lee moaned. "I'll be glad when you're done with that list. Which one gets the nod this time?"

"Ellery Queen's *The Finishing Stroke*."

"That's number nine, right?"

I nodded.

"Good," Lee said. "Just one more to go." Her voice changed inflection. "Yes, Mr. Morgan. It's Lee Holland. Remember me?"

While Lee bantered with Max Morgan, I fondly recalled the Queen novel. Written by cousins Frederic Dannay and Manfred Lee under their joint pseudonym, the book was a Christmas mystery that took Ellery twenty-seven years to solve. And, I thought, if I'm wrong about what happened to Izzy, it might even take me longer to crack this one.

"I'm sorry you feel that way," Lee was saying. "All right, good-bye."

"Bad news?" I asked.

She frowned. "I couldn't get him to budge. I even offered him an extra thousand dollars on top of the cost of his plane ticket."

"A thousand dollars?"

Lee nodded. "But it didn't do any good. He absolutely refuses to attend."

"That is a blow," I admitted.

"What do we do now?" Lee asked.

"I guess we don't have any choice," I said matter-of-factly. "We'll just have to do it without him."

CHAPTER 20

*"The author proves
he can hold his own
with anyone
in today's crowded
mystery field."*

—Stokes Moran,
on Earl Emerson's *Yellow Dog Party*

"Thank you all for coming."

Lee presided as hostess for the proceedings, though I thought I almost lost her when Tory Andrews walked in. She'd had a crush on him ever since her high school days, and suddenly here she was, face-to-face with her idol at last.

At age fifty-five, Andrews still possessed the rugged handsomeness that had made him a teenage heartthrob back in the early sixties. Arriving with him were Fairlane Jeffries, star of a long-running Western television series back in the late fifties, and Cash Hardesty, whom Lee and I had earlier interviewed in L.A. Predictably, Alexander Paxton, but unexpectedly accompanied by his wife Abigail, rang the bell precisely at ten A.M., while Toby Vickers and Mike Conover showed up a couple of minutes late.

With the group now assembled, Izzy's brownstone provided the setting. As the house had been Izzy's home for many years, no undue suspicion could be attached to its selection as the site for his final send-off. But to me it served a much more important function—as the scene of the crime. Let the guilty beware!

"I know this was an imposition for many of you," Lee apologized, "and I certainly hope you won't be disappointed." Lee paused. "What we're doing this morning is not so much a celebration of Izzy's life as it is an examination of his death." The crowd murmured its confusion. "And for further explanation, here is Kyle Malachi."

I walked to the center of the room. The seven guests were seated in a circular formation, so that they all faced me directly. I could also see each one of them clearly.

"I, too, would like to express my appreciation for your presence here today," I said. The previous day had passed as slowly as any in my entire life, so it was a relief to see the moment finally arrive. In the tradition of the great detective, I had successfully assembled the suspects together in one place. But would I also be able to catch the culprit?

"What I want to do now," I continued, "is to take you through the last few weeks of Izzy's life."

"Wait just a doggone minute," Fairlane Jeffries interrupted. "I was invited here to attend a memorial service. If you've got something else in mind, you can count me out." He rose to his feet.

"That goes double for me," said Cash Hardesty, also standing. "Let's get out of here."

"Please," I begged, panic-stricken, "don't go."

The group moved en masse toward the room's exit. "Lee," I yelled, "help!"

She stood like a castle defender at the door. "Izzy would want you to stay," she said softly, arresting their attention. "Won't you hear us out?"

Several of the men still indicated a reluctance to participate, but Abigail overrode their objections. "We've come all this way," she said, "let's at least give these children a chance to explain."

Hercule Poirot and Charlie Chan never had a roomful of suspects get up and walk out on them. What had I done wrong? Lee whispered the answer to me as the group, amid continued loud grumbling, reoccupied their seats.

"These people are not characters in a book," she said. "You've got to treat them like human beings."

Standing in the middle of a hostile semicircle, I felt helpless and exposed, a failure. Abigail once again came to the rescue.

"Young man," she advised, "why are you being so formal? Pull up a chair and we'll just sit and talk." Her smile revitalized my spirits.

"Good idea," Lee called from the side of the room, where she struggled with two more cane-back chairs. Tory Andrews jumped up to assist her, and I swear Lee almost swooned.

"Now," said Abigail, who had clearly taken the initiative, "what's this all about? And why are we the only people in attendance?"

I suddenly didn't have the least idea how to begin. So far, the morning had been a nightmare. Nothing had gone as expected, and I felt like a pitiful reject from the Hardy Boys Detective Club.

"Kyle," Lee suggested, "why don't you outline it for them the way you did for me?"

"Let's just talk," added Abigail, "like friends." Abigail's encouragement was like a lifeline in a sea of hostility.

"As many of you know," I began, somewhat hesitantly, "Izzy asked Lee and me to help him recover an item that had been taken from him. What you don't know is that I write nationally syndicated mystery reviews under the byline of Stokes Moran."

Abigail gasped. "That's wonderful," she clapped her hands. "I read your column every Sunday in the *Times*."

"What's that got to do with anything?" Alexander Paxton complained.

"Shut up, Alex," his wife scolded.

I felt a slight smile begin to grow at the corners of my lips. "Anyway, Lee convinced Izzy that I was a rather skilled amateur detective," I continued, my confidence reviving. "That's not true, of course," I admitted, "but Lee was determined to find out what was bothering Izzy. You see, he wouldn't tell her, and she couldn't stand not knowing." I shot a quick glance in Lee's direction.

"Well, Lee's lie worked, so I met with Izzy, at which time he told me that a young man named Ted Nichols—a young man who bore a striking resemblance to Lev Levin, by the way—had stolen a videotape containing, ah, certain sensitive material." Tory Andrews and Fairlane Jeffries shifted uncomfortably in their chairs. Unlike the other men present, Andrews and Jeffries had not previously been alerted about the theft.

"Izzy was only concerned about the possibility of blackmail, not of himself, but of the men featured in the videotape, sixteen of whom were known to be dead. That left ten as potential blackmail victims."

I paused. "The six of you, plus Robert Mallory, who Lee and I learned later was also dead, and Max Morgan. Plus two who now live outside the United States."

"Alex, you old rascal," Abigail hooted, "you never told me."

"Abby, be quiet," Paxton demanded. But there was no fire in his voice.

"So, at Izzy's insistence," I continued, "Lee and I agreed to fly to California to interview those of you who were still alive. But before we left New York, we first tried to track down Ted Nichols, but without success."

Tory Andrews started to say something, then seemed to change his mind.

"We talked with each of you, and, to a man, you denied that anyone had tried to extort any money from you over that tape. Lee and I were all set to return to New York where we hoped to interview you, Mr. Andrews"—I nodded in his direction—"and you, Mr. Jeffries, but Izzy's death changed our plans." Fairlane Jeffries refused to look up, choosing instead to inspect his black cowhide boots.

"Then, when I got back to my home in Connecticut, I, or rather my dog, found a dead body in the river park across from my house. It later turned out to be Ted Nichols."

Another murmur rushed through the group.

"Those are all facts." I stood up. "What comes now is speculation."

"Why should we listen to any more of this crap?" Cash Hardesty demanded. "You're making us all out to be suspects."

"You are suspects, Mr. Hardesty," I said with vehemence. "One of you is responsible for the deaths of two men."

"I'm not going to sit here and be accused of murder," he retorted. "I'm getting out of here now." Hardesty rose from his chair.

"Can we interpret your leaving," Abigail posed quietly, "as an admission of guilt?"

"How dare you!" he stammered, but he returned to his seat.

"Remember," I said, repressing a silent cheer for Abigail, "Lee had sold me to Izzy as an amateur detective. But, faced with a real-life crime, I felt totally inadequate. Then she reminded me I was a fairly astute reader of mystery fiction and that I should approach this case as if it were just another novel I was reviewing. Strangely, her suggestion worked, and I give credit to three mystery writers for helping me finally to solve the puzzle."

"This is ridiculous," said Alexander Paxton. "I'm leaving."

"Shut up, Alex," Abigail commanded. "Nobody's going anywhere. Please continue, young man."

"The first was Sir Arthur Conan Doyle," I said. "Sherlock Holmes' dictum was always that once you eliminate the impossible, whatever's left, no matter how improbable, must be the truth.

"Second was Agatha Christie, whose book *Curtain*"—here I smiled at Lee—"suggested certain similarities. In that novel, the villain never actually kills anyone, but he creates situations where murder is a natural outcome.

"Third, the title for one of Earl Emerson's Mac Fontana stories—*Morons and Madmen*—made me realize that perhaps I wasn't up against a brilliant adversary, merely a stupid one." I paused, watching to see if the insult elicited any response. It didn't.

"In any criminal investigation," I said, taking a step to my right, "three things have to be established—means, motive, and opportunity. While all three are important, in this particular case I felt the key factor was the motive. If I could identify that, I believed I could solve the case."

I stopped pacing. "The motive," I said with emotion, "was greed. Basic, old-fashioned, no-holds-barred naked avarice." I let my listeners absorb those words.

"Izzy's death appeared to be from natural causes. The preliminary finding at the scene of the crime was that he died from a ruptured thoracic aorta, brought on by a lifetime history of hypertension.

NEIL McGAUGHEY

"But there were complications to that theory. For one, not only was there blood where his body was discovered, blood was also found in the elevator, the third-floor hallway, and even in Izzy's bedroom. Certainly, too much blood to be from natural causes.

"And," I paused dramatically, "a bullet hole was found in the frame of Izzy's bed. Not a bullet, or a gun, just a bullet hole.

"The New York police were at a loss to explain what had happened. They had a dead body that showed no evidence of trauma, enough blood to fill the Central Park Reservoir, and a bullet hole, but no bullet or gun to go along with it.

"Then a dead Ted Nichols turned up virtually on my doorstep, with a bullet hole in his head. Coincidence?" I shook my head. "No way."

Toby Vickers moved restlessly. "My first thought was that Nichols learned I was looking for him and was on his way to see me when he was killed. But that didn't hold water." I grimaced. "I'm sorry. Since the body was found in the river, that was a bad pun."

I continued. "Plus the logical assumption is that the bullet hole in Izzy's bed and the bullet hole in Nichols' head must be connected."

"Were they?" Abigail interrupted, then apologized. "I'm sorry."

I smiled. "Of course they were. But how? And where was the gun that had made them?"

I let my audience consider those questions, then I said, "It looked like an impossible puzzle. Izzy was dead, supposedly by natural causes. Ted Nichols was dead, shot in the head. That's when I finally realized the motive."

Lee coughed, tapping her watch. Speed it up, she was telling me.

"Izzy did die of natural causes, just as it appeared. Brought on not by hypertension but by the extreme exertion of dragging a dead man halfway through his house."

Everyone nervously moved in their chairs, but only Abigail spoke. "You mean—" she started.

"Yes," I confirmed, "Izzy Cohen killed Ted Nichols."

"I don't believe it," sputtered Cash Hardesty. "That's a bunch of crap."

"No, it's not," I said. "It's the only explanation that makes any sense. Ted Nichols bore an uncanny resemblance to Lev Levin. Izzy told me himself that he'd never been able to resist Lev, and Nichols had the same effect on him."

I could see a dawning realization in Abigail's eyes. "Something bothered me about Izzy's assignment from the outset. Izzy was not at all concerned about that videotape being reproduced. Lee and I immediately felt that its commercial value was the primary motivation for its theft. We even checked to see if it had been offered for sale. But Izzy was only concerned with the potential blackmail threat it posed to his former clients. Why?"

The audience held its collective breath. "I can only guess at the answer," I said. "Lev Levin was a skilled technician, so—"

"He booby-trapped the tape," Abigail supplied, then covered her mouth with her hands.

"That's as good a way to describe it as any," I acknowledged. "Izzy knew the tape couldn't be copied, so all he wanted from Lee and me was confirmation that you men weren't being victimized. And, if he had lived, that's what he would have gotten. As Izzy saw it, everything would have been fine. Except for one thing." I paused again. "Ted Nichols showed up at his doorstep, and this time he had come after the films themselves.

"The tape had been destroyed. The person behind all this was desperate for the money the films represented. Izzy, knowing that sooner or later Ted Nichols would wear away his resistance, did the only thing he believed would keep those films from going public. He killed Ted Nichols and, in the process, died from his efforts."

"But what happened to the gun?" Abigail demanded.

"The man who brought Ted Nichols to Izzy's house that night took it," I answered.

"Why?" she asked.

"I suppose he thought if he helped Izzy out of this jam, then Izzy might give him the films after all."

"What do you mean, if he helped Izzy? Wasn't Izzy dead?"

"No, I don't believe so," I speculated. "I think the man waited outside the house while Ted Nichols was here, after a few hours probably became impatient, and went to investigate. I believe he found Izzy, still alive, dragging Nichols' body across the front hall. He then took the body to my place and possibly threw the gun in the river."

"But why would he risk taking the body all the way out to Connecticut?" Abigail made a wonderful foil; she asked all the right questions. I'd have to remember to invite her to my next murder party.

"Because he knew I wasn't home. You see, Lee had conveniently provided each of you with our home addresses. The killer, and I will continue to call him a killer even though technically and unfortunately legally he didn't kill anyone, thought he'd dump the body somewhere on my property where no one would see him but where the body would easily be seen in the daylight. But when he got out to my house, he found I lived at the end of a cul-de-sac where it would be too risky to get in and out without being seen. His second option was to drop the body in the river across from where I lived, assuming it would be discovered the next day, certainly well before I returned from California.

"You see, if I heard upon my return a body had been found in the neighborhood, I'd think it unusual but I certainly wouldn't go down to the morgue to look at it. And that was what our man was most concerned with."

I walked forward, standing directly in front of one of the men. "It was just his bad luck that the following day was so cold that no one ventured into the park, and even further bad luck that I have a normal routine of running with my dog every morning in that park. Once I saw the body, it was just a matter of time before I'd connect Ted Nichols with our killer."

"Why is that?" asked Abigail.

"You see, he knew I, or I should say we, had something that could link him indisputably to the murdered man. Lee, in fact, had stolen it right out from under his nose."

I looked down. "Isn't that right, Mr. Conover?"

CHAPTER 21

"The novel never blinks
at exposing
the most appalling of
human
vices and weaknesses."

—Stokes Moran,
on James Ellroy's *L.A. Confidential*

*M*ike Conover sat unmoving, stiff and silent. Would he refuse to talk? Would he get up and walk out? Would he sue me for defamation of character?

Or would he talk?

"I didn't kill anybody," he finally said. And I knew I had him.

"How could I?" he suddenly posed, with renewed animation. "I was in L.A. when it happened. You know that, you saw me."

"You attempted to establish an alibi by showing up at our hotel on the morning following the murder," I answered. "But you had not come directly from your apartment as you wanted us to believe, but straight from the airport, where you had only recently arrived on a midnight flight from New York."

"You can't prove that," he challenged.

"You're right. I can't," I agreed, "because I'm sure you flew back into L.A. under an assumed name. But I can prove that you and Edward Nichols flew to New York the previous day." I pulled a folded passenger manifest out of my jacket pocket, shook it open, and held the paper out for him to inspect.

"Once I knew you were the killer," I said, "it wasn't hard for a friend of mine to turn this up. You see, you had no reason to conceal your identity on the first flight because you had no idea anything bad was about to happen. Even Nichols was booked under his real name."

Conover sagged. "In all the time we were attempting to locate Ted Nichols, it never occurred to either Lee or me that Ted can also be a nickname for Edward. And when I read down that list of names on the *Bosun Buddies* box, I sailed right past the name Nick Edwards, even though you yourself told me actors in x-rated films often change their names around. Ted Nichols, Nick Edwards, Edward Nichols. All the same guy."

"I never killed anybody," Conover repeated. "It's not right that you say I did. All I wanted was those films."

"You were the only one of Izzy's clients who knew of the existence of films other than your own," I said. "Izzy even wrote in his notes to Lee and me that you had once viewed some of the other films, but we were too half-witted at the time to understand the importance of that fact." I laughed. "You even told us as much when you said you were the last letter in Izzy's alphabet. Only you knew there were twenty-six men on that tape." I laughed. "There you were, giving me the most important clue of all, and I just blindly passed it by."

"That tape was worth millions," he said. "Lev had done a beautiful job editing it, real professional. I couldn't believe it when it self-destructed."

"You were desperate for money," I suggested. "You were getting a little too old for the business you were in, so you remembered those films of Izzy's and realized the potential."

"You just don't know," he admitted. "Nothing like that tape has ever been available before. Twenty-six of Hollywood's all-time biggest studs. You think that Rob Lowe videotape caused a stir, this one would have knocked the roof off. The crossover market would have been amazing. Even little old ladies, hot for some of these guys since the early fifties, would have bought this thing. We're talking fifty, hundred million easy. U.S. dollars."

"And the fact that two men are dead because of your greed means absolutely nothing," I said.

Conover stood up. "Look, I didn't mean for any of that to happen. The minute I saw Ted, I realized he was a dead ringer for Lev. At first, I just thought it would be nice to eventually introduce him to Izzy. But later, when I remembered those films, I got the idea of using him to get them away from Izzy. I didn't even know about the videotape at the time."

"And you brought Nichols to New York, followed Izzy around for a while until you picked your moment, and then allowed Nichols just to accidentally bump into Izzy at the Rainbow Room," I prodded.

"You make it sound so cold," he said. "But that's basically right."

"And you told him not to let on that he knew anybody in those films."

"I told him he should drop hints about the famous men he'd been with, knowing sooner or later Izzy would trot out his own collection," he answered. "I cautioned Ted if that should happen, he had to play dumb about the men he might see on those films, knowing Izzy's ego would never stand for that. After all, those films were like his trophies. If he thought Ted wasn't interested, then he'd go all out trying to impress him. Maybe even get careless in the process.

"Oh, yes," he said, smiling. "It worked. When he came back to L.A. with that videotape, I thought I'd died and gone to heaven. It was everything I'd hoped for, and more. But then, when I tried to duplicate it, the damn thing self-destructed."

Conover looked so forlorn, I almost felt sorry for him. Almost, but not quite.

"Then what happened?" I asked.

"I didn't know what to do," he said. "I knew we couldn't go back to Izzy; we'd already burned that bridge. I started dreaming of ways to steal the films. Until you showed up." He glared at me.

"When you gave me Izzy's gift, I realized I had run out of time. If he was giving me my film back, then he was doing the same thing for the other guys.

"As soon as you left my apartment, I got in touch with Ted and told him we had to get to New York fast and that he'd

just have to face Izzy again and try to convince Izzy to take
him back. Then, once he had Izzy purring like a kitten,
maybe Ted could swipe the safety deposit keys and I could
nab the films."

"But it didn't happen like that," I prompted.

"No, it went terribly wrong." Conover cradled his head in
his hands. "I rented a car at the airport, knowing I couldn't
just stand outside Izzy's door while Ted took care of business. I sat in that car for over four hours, the last hour absolutely convinced something bad had happened. Finally, I
got up enough nerve to go see." He stopped.

"And when you entered the house, you found Ted's body."

He nodded. "The front door was unlocked. I just turned the
knob and it opened right up. And there was Izzy, dragging
Ted's body across the floor. He looked at me and knew immediately why I was there. He told me I should be ashamed of
myself, him with a dead body on his hands, and he was lecturing me." Conover laughed. "I couldn't believe it."

I walked back toward the fireplace. "Did he ask you to
dispose of the body?"

"He didn't ask me nothing," Conover answered. "He told
me to get rid of Ted, and he handed me the gun as well."

"The thirty-eight Webley?"

"I don't know what kind of gun it was. Izzy said something about Lev bringing it back from the war, but I don't
remember if he ever said what kind it was. Anyway, I lifted
Ted up in my arms, draped a blanket Izzy gave me around
the body so in case anybody saw they'd think Ted was just

sick, and carried him out to the car, without the least idea of what to do with him. Then I remembered I had that piece of paper your girlfriend had handed me. I pulled that out of my billfold, saw that her address wouldn't work because it was in Manhattan, but that yours might."

"But when you got out there—" I left the sentence unfinished.

"Man, I had an awful time finding your place. Then, when I finally did get there, it was a dead-end street. I couldn't risk driving back to New York with Ted still in the car, so I just dumped him in the river. I thought surely somebody would find his body the next day."

"Then when you got back to Izzy's place—" I felt like I was playing fill in the blanks.

"There were cop cars and ambulances and people standing around on the sidewalk. I asked one guy what had happened and he said some old man had died. Well, I knew what that meant so I hightailed it to the airport, threw my return ticket away, and bought a standby with a made-up name. On the flight home, I thought up the idea of meeting up with you at your hotel so you'd believe I'd been in L.A. the whole time."

"It almost worked, too," I acknowledged.

"Man, I didn't kill anybody," he said again, almost crying.

"Two men are dead who would otherwise still be alive if not for your greed," I said. "Don't you think that's the same as murder?"

He frantically shook his head, stifling a sob.

"Well, the police can't touch you," I said. "The only thing I believe you could be charged with is accessory after the fact, and for that to happen, we'd have to drag Izzy's name through the mud. And I'm not willing to do that." I looked toward Lee. "Neither is my future wife. So I guess we'll just quietly explain what happened to the local police and hope they'll close the case. I have a friend who assures me they will."

"You mean I'm free to go?" Conover asked.

"I certainly can't detain you," I answered.

He rose to leave. "What'll happen to those films?" he asked. "There's enough money to be made that we all could be rich."

Something inside me snapped though my voice remained calm.

"Well, I guess that's up to us," I answered. "I think we all have a vested interest in the status of those films. Don't you, everybody?"

The other members of the group, who had remained docilely quiet during my entire confrontation with Conover, suddenly erupted into voice. I shouted over the melee.

"This is as close as you'll come to a jury trial," I yelled. "We're not quite twelve, but I'm willing to abide by our decision. What do we do with the films?" I polled the audience. "Sell 'em or burn 'em?"

In unison, everyone but Conover shouted back, "Burn 'em."

"I guess that's your answer." I spoke in a more normal

tone since the furor had lessened. Conover walked out of the room with all the semblance of a man on the way to the gallows, a clearly defeated adversary. Why didn't I feel more vindicated? Then again, maybe some justice had been served after all.

The other members of the memorial service filed out after him. Only Abigail stopped to say anything. "Hell of a morning," she commented with a wink.

When Lee and I were once again alone in the room, she walked over to me.

"Don't you think you were a little hard on Conover?"

"He deserved it," I said. "If he hadn't been so greedy, two men would still be alive."

"But when you stop and think about it," she said, "he had basically given up on the scheme until we showed up at his L.A. apartment and told him Izzy was getting ready to destroy the films."

"You told him that," I reminded her.

She ignored my subterfuge. "You know what I'm getting at. You say Conover set things in motion." Lee paused, then added sadly, "You could make the same claim against us."

I thought about what she had said. Where is the responsibility? Where does guilt truly lie? Maybe we must all share the blame, even the dead.

"No," I disagreed. "No matter how you look at it, Conover is the one responsible. If it hadn't been for him, Nichols never would have stolen the tape and Izzy never would have come to us. So," I judged, "Conover's to blame for all of it."

Suddenly, Lee threw her arms around me and hugged my neck. "Let's just forget all of that for the time being. Isn't it wonderful? You were right. Your theory held up. Kyle, I'm proud of you. You're a regular Sam Spade," she said, laughing.

I smiled. "Maybe I wouldn't make such a bad amateur detective after all."

"Bad? You were magnificent."

"Well, I wouldn't go that far," I said. "Remember, I was pretty miserable there at the beginning. If you hadn't stopped them, everybody would have walked out."

"You were just too stern," she said. "I think you scared them."

"I scared them? You didn't see how my knees were shaking."

Lee laughed. "Well, you did fine. There's just one thing you didn't share with me. How did you know about the make of the gun?"

"Nolan looked it up for me," I answered. "Once he'd confirmed what I suspected—that Lev had shot himself—I asked him to find out if either Izzy or Lev had ever registered a gun. Lev had, a souvenir he had brought back with him from World War Two, as Conover stated."

I slowly slid my left arm around Lee's waist and guided her toward the front door. "You know, Nolan tells me the reason the police never found the bullet is that Lev brought back from the war, in addition to the gun itself, some armor-piercing shells that can shoot right through hardened steel."

Lee frowned. "How can Nolan know what Lev did or didn't bring back from the Second World War?"

I grinned. "You don't want me to give away all Nolan's secrets, do you?"

"Yes, I do."

"All right," I said, "but you're not going to like it. Nolan found Lev's diary."

Lee stopped in mid-stride. "Now, how did he do that?"

"Yesterday, while you and I were otherwise occupied, he sort of borrowed the keys you got from Izzy's lawyer and went through all of Izzy's safety deposit boxes."

"What!" Lee exploded. "I'll kill him."

"Calm down," I soothed. "Anyway, he did it at my direction."

"Why?" she demanded, still angry.

"I couldn't take a chance on those films winding up in Conover's hands, now could I?"

"You mean—"

"Already ashes."

Lee shook her head. "If only it could have been that simple for Izzy."

I nodded. "When it came down to it," I said, "he found it easier to take a life than to destroy a few strips of celluloid."

"I still don't understand it," she said. "Izzy was the kindest, most gentle man I ever knew. Never would I have believed him capable of killing anything, let alone a human being." Lee paused, then added, "and yet he did."

"People will surprise you," I admitted. "Mystery novels and true crime stories wouldn't exist at all if it weren't for all those least-likely suspects turning out to be murderers."

"Where's Lev's diary now?" Lee asked, holding out her hand as if expecting me to produce it from thin air.

"Nolan's still got it," I said. Then I grinned. "He says it's fascinating reading."

"I bet. Just what other little tidbits has Nolan unearthed?"

"Well," I drawled, "now that you ask."

"You don't mean there's something else?" Lee objected. "Talk about deus ex machina. If this were a mystery novel, no reader would buy it." She frowned, waiting for me to speak. "Well, go on, out with it."

"Lev also detailed how he sabotaged the tape," I answered.

"Nolan just conveniently stumbled on that information," Lee protested. "Are there any other loose ends that need to be tidied up?" She paused. "Okay, I'm waiting. How'd Lev do it?"

"It seems," I explained, "that Lev inserted a magnet into the videotape and a screw into Izzy's machine. When the tape was played in Izzy's VCR, everything was fine, the screw lifted the magnet away from the tape. But—"

"I get you," Lee interrupted. "If the tape was played on any other machine, the magnet would lie against the tape and erase it."

I nodded. "It could be watched once," I added, "but as it was being played, it was also being erased."

"Ingenious," Lee said sarcastically. "When do I get to read this remarkable diary?"

"It should be out in paperback by next spring," I kidded. "You'll just have to wait until then."

Lee laughed. "Fine," she said. "Just so long as I get the agent's commission."

"Oh, absolutely."

Lee walked with me to the door. "Were you serious about being able to keep this all quiet?"

"Nolan's talked to the police, both here and in Tipton. They seem satisfied that all their questions have been answered and agree that no justice would be served in going public with any of it, at least not at this point anyway."

"In that case," she said, "I might be willing to forgive you for taking those safety deposit box keys." Lee laughed, then added, "in about five or ten years."

"That long? I completed my all-time favorite mysteries list in much less time than that."

"What's tha—" she began, then said, "you mean it's finally finished?"

I nodded.

"Well, what's the last entry?"

"A title that I think is very appropriate for the case we've just finished," I said. "And I didn't pick it just for its title. It's one of the best mysteries I've ever read."

"So quit stalling. What is it?"

I smiled. "Sarah Caudwell's wonderful first novel," I answered finally. *"Thus Was Adonis Murdered."*

Lee laughed. "You're right," she said. "That selection aptly crowns this whole process. I'm just glad you're finally done with that interminable list."

"Yes," I agreed. "Or, if I might misquote the great Agatha Christie—"

I paused, then added with a flourish, "And Then There Were Ten."

CHAPTER 22

*"The reader is
willingly and gloriously
transported
into the author's world."*

—Stokes Moran,
on Nevada Barr's *Track of the Cat*

$\mathcal{L}$ess than a month later, on February seventeenth, in the Tipton municipal court chambers of Judge Wanda Walmsley, Lee Holland added Malachi to her list of legal names. For better or worse.

Bootsie served as maid of honor.

A F T E R W O R D

*F*or the meticulous reader, here is a convenient recap of Stokes Moran's ten all-time favorite mysteries (in chronological order of American publication):

The Hound of the Baskervilles, Sir Arthur Conan Doyle
Farewell, My Lovely, Raymond Chandler
The Finishing Stroke, Ellery Queen
The List of Adrian Messenger, Philip MacDonald
Curtain, Agatha Christie
The Affair of the Blood-Stained Egg Cosy, James Anderson
Edwin of the Iron Shoes, Marcia Muller
Thus Was Adonis Murdered, Sarah Caudwell
A Little Class on Murder, Carolyn G. Hart
Devil in a Blue Dress, Walter Mosley

ABOUT THE AUTHOR

Neil McGaughey reviews mysteries for *The Clarion-Ledger* in Jackson, Mississippi. He is a member of the Mystery Writers of America and Sisters-in-Crime.

His first Stokes Moran mystery, *Otherwise Known as Murder*, was published by Scribner in 1994. He is currently at work on the third installment in the Stokes Moran series.